PLANET OF THE APES

NOVELIZATION

by

John Whitman

Based on the motion picture screenplay written by
William Broyles, Jr., and
Lawrence Konner
& Mark D. Rosenthal

PUFFIN BOOKS

PUFFIN BOOKS

Penguin Books Ltd, 27 Wrights Lane, London W8 5TZ, England
Penguin Putnam Inc., 375 Hudson Street, New York, New York 10014, USA
Penguin Books Australia Ltd, Ringwood, Victoria, Australia
Penguin Books Canada Ltd, 10 Alcorn Avenue, Toronto, Ontario, Canada M4V 3B2
Penguin Books India (P) Ltd, 11 Community Centre, Panchsheel Park,
New Delhi – 110 017, India
Penguin Books (NZ) Ltd, Cnr Rosedale and Airborne Roads, Albany,
Auckland, New Zealand
Penguin Books (South Africa) (Pty) Ltd, 5 Watkins Street, Denver Ext 4,
Johannesburg 2094, South Africa

On the World Wide Web at: www.penguin.com

Penguin Books Ltd, Registered Offices: Harmondsworth, Middlesex, England

First published in the US by HarperEntertainment, an imprint of
HarperCollins Publishers, Inc., 2001
Published in Great Britain in Puffin Books, 2001

1

Set in 11.75 on 15pt New Baskerville

Made and printed in England by Clays Ltd, St Ives plc

British Library Cataloguing in Publication Data
A CIP catalogue record for this book is available from the British Library

ISBN 0-141-31376-5

CHAPTER ONE

The flight pod bucked as it skimmed the edge of Jupiter's gravity well. The pilot leaned forward and slapped a control lever with the lazy confidence of someone who'd followed the routine a hundred times. The turbulence subsided.

The pilot tugged at the monitoring vest strapped to his chest. Comfortable with navigational procedures, he was just as *un*comfortable with the uniform. They had never been able to find one that fit him right.

An alarm on the control panel bleeped, and a round sphere blossomed at the center of the flight pod's view screen. The pilot had been too busy learning command procedures to remember the name of this celestial object. Vaguely, he recalled a phrase and a name uttered by people back on the command ship. *Moon of Jupiter. Europa.*

On cue, the pilot entered a new series of commands designed to stop the alarm sound. But instead of stopping, the alarm grew louder, and a blinking light flashed on the control panel. The pilot grunted and reentered the command sequence. The alarm grew more urgent.

The pilot leaned forward anxiously. As he did, his face fell into the light of the alarm beacon and was reflected in the view screen. His face was framed by thick dark hair. His dark round eyes stared intently down at the control panel, and the nostrils on his flat nose flared nervously.

He was a handsome chimpanzee.

The chimp pilot showed his teeth in a nervous grin and carefully punched the keys in the order he'd memorized so carefully, but still the flight pod would not respond. With another, louder grunt, the pilot slapped the controls in frustration. The pod bucked and swerved as though it had been grabbed by a giant hand. It was heading straight for Europa now, and the Jovian moon was swelling in the view screen.

The pilot screamed and began to pound at the controls helplessly. He threw one hand up over his eyes to block out the view of the moon rushing toward him while the other continued to slap the panel meaninglessly.

At the last second before the pod hurtled down into Europa's grip, another hand reached over the chimp's shoulder and touched a lone button on the control panel. All at once the alarms ceased. The view screen froze, and the cabin lights went up.

Capt. Leo Davidson, late twenties, and carrying himself with the confidence of a man who'd spent a career navigating the hostile environment of space, slid up alongside the chimp pilot. On the screen, a text message popped up. SIMULATION PAUSED. END PROGRAM? Y/N.

Leo ended the program and then smiled at the chimp. "Sorry, Pericles. You lose."

The chimp looked back at him and chattered indignantly.

"Surprised?" the human laughed. "I changed your flight sequence."

Pericles tapped the keys. *Changed the flight sequence.* He understood that that meant a different order of buttons, an order he hadn't been taught. It wasn't fair.

"I know you can hit the fastball . . . but what about the curve?"

In response, Pericles curled his lip like a toddler and smashed his hand down on the console. *Bam!*

Leo frowned. "That's enough, Pericles."

Bam!

"Stop it . . ."

Bam!"

". . . or no treat."

Pericles stopped and folded his long-fingered hands into his lap.

Leo laughed. "How well do I know you? Come on, let's get out of this place."

Leo and Pericles left the flight simulation deck of the United States Air Force *Oberon*. *Oberon* was the latest success in a series of rapid-fire advancements in technology that had energized the space program after nearly a century of neglect. The ship was currently in orbit about twenty-five miles above Earth's surface.

As Leo and Pericles exited the simulator and walked down one gleaming white hall, the human ran his hand along the hull.

What a waste. About two hundred billion dollars' worth of research and construction to create a ship that could fly to Jupiter and back, and *Oberon* spent most of her time tethered to Earth by politicians brave enough to build expensive toys but too scared to actually play with them. Leo spent his downtime imagining what he'd do with five minutes at the helm of *Oberon*.

Oberon was a model of quiet efficiency and order. That was, until you reached the Animal Living Quarters. Leo and Pericles reached the door and barely glanced at the warning sign announcing—CAUTION: LIVE ANIMALS. SECURITY ACCESS ONLY.

Leo keyed the entry and the door slid back. Instantly he was assaulted by a riot of hoots and shrieks. Pericles grabbed Leo's hand instinctively; then he released it a moment later as the sounds registered as mostly joyful and anxious. The primates on *Oberon* were treated with care.

Leo passed by an orangutan in a large cage. The primate's wide, intent eyes studied a mock-up of the same control panel Pericles had worked in the flight simulator. The orangutan was slowly inputting sequences in response to signals on the screen. Every time he punched in the right code, he'd be rewarded with a mango.

In another section of the Animal Quarters, a technician was sampling a melody on a small keyboard. Beside him, a lowland gorilla stared quizzically at the keyboard, listening to the melody intently. When the technician stopped playing, the gorilla reached out tentatively and tapped the keys, reproducing the melody slowly and perfectly.

Suddenly Pericles scooted forward and leaped into the waiting arms of a young woman in a white lab coat adorned by a pair of glasses hanging from a neck-strap and a badge that read Lt. Col. Grace Alexander, Chief Medical Officer.

Dr. Alexander nuzzled Pericles' face. "Was the *Homo sapiens* mean to you again?" She glanced at Leo disapprovingly. "We all know it's just rocket envy."

Leo grinned back at her. Grace Alexander was a couple of years older than he was, probably smarter than he was, and she certainly outranked him. All of which put her at the center of his attention. He pointed to the chimp she was hugging so closely in her arms. "You ever consider getting an actual boyfriend?"

"You mean do I enjoy being miserable?" the chief medical officer shot back. "I'll stick with my chimps."

Pericles tugged at the doctor's coat, wanting something. When she didn't respond, he jumped out of her arms and onto a nearby counter and began to tug at a locked cabinet, chattering impatiently. Leo popped the cabinet open and scooped a biscuit out of a huge bag of treats. But instead of passing it to Pericles' outstretched hand, he held the biscuit behind his back.

"Which hand?" he asked.

The chimpanzee shot him a look that, in a human, would have amounted to an insult. Then he jabbed at Leo's left hand. The captain brought that hand up. Empty. Pericles pointed to the other hand and Leo brought it up. Empty. The chimpanzee squawked in frustration.

Leo sighed. "Another curve."

He reached behind his back and pulled the biscuit from his pocket. He tossed it to Pericles, who caught it in midair and hopped a few feet away as though Leo might suddenly try to snatch it back.

Dr. Alexander's eyes turned to Leo with sudden seriousness. "You weren't authorized to change his flight training."

Leo shrugged. "I'm teaching him."

Dr. Alexander refused to be dismissed. "You're teasing him. It's not the same thing."

Leo Davidson didn't have a Ph.D. in molecular biology, nor was he an expert on primate behavior. But he was a captain in the United States Air Force space exploration division. He'd flown a dozen midrange space missions before the age of thirty, and he was top man on the *Oberon*'s flight list. He certainly wasn't going to back down from a doctor, no matter how good-looking she was. He met her gaze with a self-assured smile.

"That monkey is gene-spliced, chromosome enhanced . . . He's a state-of-the-art primate. He can take it."

Dr. Alexander replied, "When you frustrate them, they lose focus, they get confused. Even violent."

Leo jabbed his finger toward the bulkhead of the ship. "Out there it's frustrating. Out there you can get confused, and if that happens, you don't have a chance to get violent because you get dead. I like Pericles, Doc, and I want him to come back from every mission he goes on. That's why I changed his training program."

"I would simply appreciate it if you'd—"

A new shriek erupted from a nearby cage, and a pair of simian hands grabbed hold of the bars, rattling them with surprising strength. Pericles loped over to the cage and put his long fingers over the hands of the chimp inside. She was a female with a round belly. She hooted at Pericles softly and he chittered back.

Dr. Alexander could not suppress a smile. "Congratulations, Pericles, you're going to be a daddy."

Leo raised an eyebrow. "Really? I thought I saw a smirk on his face."

"Actually," said the doctor with a smirk of her own, "the female was the aggressive one."

"Chimps have all the luck," Leo joked. But when he glanced at Dr. Alexander he realized she was looking at him meaningfully, and he wondered if he'd just missed his chance to ask her out.

"Captain Davidson. Postcard!" A noncommissioned officer passed by, handing Leo a thin LCD mini computer monitor about the size of his palm. He looked back at the doctor, hoping to get a little more of that look she'd been giving him, but the moment had passed, and she turned away. Leo made a mental note to kick himself later.

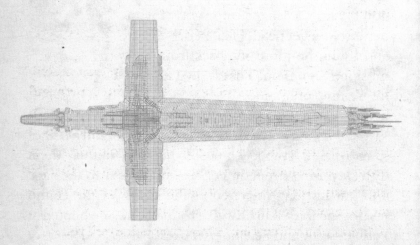

CHAPTER TWO

Leo found a quiet spot in the rear section of the ship, leaned back against the bulkhead, and clicked the postcard into play. The date flashed quickly. 02-07-2029. Nearly a week ago. The mail was slow in outer space.

For a moment the screen was filled with a heaving beige blur, until the video zoomed out and Leo realized it was his father's forehead. His mother, sister, and younger brother were all crammed into the frame, with other relatives flashing in and out of the chaotic background.

"Now?" his mother said, a bit flustered. "Okay. Hi, Leo! It's Mom."

"Hi, Leo!" "Hi, nephew!" "Keep your helmet sealed, buddy!" A wave of faces washed onto the tiny screen and then fell back until he saw only his mother and father. In the background he could see bits of an old airstrip, a hangar, and a wind sock hanging from a pole. He recognized it as the local airport where he'd taken his first flying lesson—his home away from home before joining the air force and then the space division.

"Leo," his mother said, "I have so much to tell you . . ."

His father cleared his throat and spoke up. "But she won't, son, 'cause this is costing me a fortune. Hi, Leo. The TV showed some pictures of you from space*zzzztttt*—" The screen sputtered for a moment, then snapped back and his father was saying "—real proud of you—"

pzzzztttt.

The transmission cut out again; then Leo caught a glimpse of his mother smiling against a tear and saying, "We just want you to come back to us safely—"

ppszzzzt-pop!

The picture cut out completely, replaced by static.

"Hey," Leo complained. He tapped the postcard and then smacked it against the bulkhead. The static was replaced by a black background and the words YOUR SERVICE HAS BEEN INTERRUPTED.

"No kidding," Leo snorted. "We can build a starship with nuclear fuel cells designed to last forever, but we can't—"

Suddenly, the hallway lights went out. In fact, every light on the ship went out. For a moment, the slightest moment, Leo felt fear seep through his usually courageous outlook. He waved his hand in front of his face and saw nothing.

A moment later, an emergency generator whined to life and the lights came back on. Leo sighed with relief and bolted for the command deck. Something was seriously wrong.

CHAPTER THREE

An elevator door slid open, and Leo dashed down one of *Oberon*'s many corridors. This one ended in a large wall made of shatter-proof glass. Set into the transparent wall was a control panel and a scanning screen. Leo pressed his hand against the screen, which flashed briefly. A door in the glass wall opened and Leo rushed inside.

A number of crew members were already there. He glanced at Dr. Alexander, then gave a nod to Hansen, a tech specialist, and two of the ship's officers: Maj. Frank Santos and Maria Cooper. Karl Vasich, the ship's commander, paced back and forth anxiously as his crew studied a number of displays.

"We found it," Santos said. Commander Vasich stopped pacing.

"It found us," Maria Cooper corrected. She pointed up at the ship's main view screen.

On the screen Leo saw a cloud, a mix of dark and light like a storm head lit up by sunrise, rushing through space.

"It's moving like a storm," Hansen, the techie, said.

Commander Vasich nodded. "That's what it is. An electromagnetic storm."

Major Santos looked at his screen to confirm something. "That's what's causing blackouts on Earth."

"It's . . . it's beautiful," Maria Cooper said reluctantly.

Vasich smirked. "So's the sun till you get too close."

"This is weird," Hansen muttered.

"Could you be a little less technical?" Leo asked.

Hansen explained. "I'm picking up frequency patterns. All across the band. Radio waves, television signals, the works."

"Tune them in," Commander Vasich ordered.

The technician opened up his receiver and switched the signal from his headset to the main screen. Instantly the command deck was filled with sights and sounds flashing onto the screen. Leo caught images of an old black-and-white cartoon, a big purple dinosaur, a music video with a very young-looking Madonna, a broadcast of the first moon walk, and some modern television shows that Leo liked to watch.

"What is all that?" Major Santos asked.

"That . . . thing is sucking up satellite relays," Hansen explained, although he hardly seemed to believe himself. "It's picking up satellites, cell phone conversations, TV broadcasts . . . every electronic communication from Earth . . ."

"But some of those broadcasts are twenty, thirty years old," the commander said.

"Yeah," Leo agreed. "I haven't seen that Madonna video since I was a kid."

"I know . . . ," Hansen said. "It's picking up broadcasts from . . . from all time."

"That's a lot of TV." Leo smirked. "Ten billion channels and nothing to watch."

The first bleep of an alarm sounded and then went silent. At the same moment, the entire ship went dark again. When the power returned, and they all stared at each other nervously.

"It sure knows how to get your attention," Maria Cooper whispered.

Commander Vasich was the first to recover his wits. "All right. Let's get to work." Leo was impressed with how businesslike he made it sound. "We'll start with a pass through the core. Take initial radiation and gamma ray readings." He nodded at Leo. "Get your monkey ready."

Leo hesitated. "Uh, sir, this is a waste of time."

The other officers groaned. Vasich rolled his eyes. "Captain Davidson, we have standard procedures—"

"And by the time you go through all of them, that electromagnetic storm could be gone."

Vasich knew what his ace pilot was lobbying for, and he was prepared for it. "No manned flights," he said, quoting right from the mission guidelines. "First we send out an ape. Then if it's safe, we send a pilot. No exceptions."

Thirty minutes later Leo was standing next to the pilot's seat in *Alpha Pod*, strapping Pericles in. He worked hard to hide his nervousness from the chimp. That was the most difficult part of Leo's job, but he knew that Pericles' life depended on it. If Pericles detected fear in Leo, he'd start to become afraid himself, and that might make him forget all his careful training.

"Okay, pal," Leo said, patting Pericles on the head. "Just follow your sequence and then come home. Understand? *Home.*"

Leo stepped back. Pericles screeched once. To reassure him, Leo gave a thumbs-up sign. The chimp looked down at his own hand, selected his thumb, and raised it. Leo grinned and kept the smile on his face until the pod door was completely sealed.

It took Leo no more than ninety seconds to sprint back to the command deck. He plopped down at the station, elbow-to-elbow with Commander Vasich, and slid on the headset.

"Pod away," droned a neutral voice from somewhere in the ship.

"Acknowledged," Commander Vasich said. A timer on the command console begin to tick away the seconds.

On his own console, Leo tracked *Alpha Pod*'s flight path as it looped once around the much larger *Oberon* and then streaked away toward the electromagnetic storm. For a few brief seconds, *Alpha Pod*'s flight looked picture perfect. Then the image started to blink.

"What's wrong?" a soft voice said breathlessly.

Leo nearly jumped. He hadn't realized that Dr. Alexander was leaning over his shoulder.

"The blink indicates he's off course," Leo said.

Vasich's businesslike voice continued. "Lock on him."

"He's not responding," Leo said.

Dr. Alexander's eyes shifted to the medical readouts transmitted by the vest Pericles wore. "There's a surge in his heart rate. He's scared."

Leo tried to boost the signal, hoping Perciles would catch it and make the changes he wanted. But instead of smoothing out, the indicator showing the chimp's course began to blink more rapidly; then it simply went out.

Leo's breath caught in his throat. He waited, expecting the indicator to come back on. Then he waited, expecting someone to say there'd been a malfunction. But there was nothing wrong with the equipment, and the light did not return.

"We lost him," Leo breathed.

"Light him up again," Vasich ordered.

"I can't," Leo said in the same shocked whisper. "Jesus . . . he's gone."

He felt Grace Alexander's hand touch his shoulder reassuringly. "He's trained to come back to the *Oberon*."

Leo ignored her and spun toward Vasich. He stared at

the commander wordlessly for a moment and then said, "I'm waiting for orders, sir."

Commander Vasich knew what Leo meant. Everyone in the *room* knew what Leo meant. They all watched as Vasich sat back in his seat, weighing his better judgment against his admiration for Leo's loyalty and courage. Finally, his jaw stiff, the commander growled, "We sit tight for now and wait."

Leo tensed up, but he swallowed the protest that nearly burst from his lips. Instead he slowly stood up and straightened his flight suit. "I'll . . . I'll run some sequences in *Delta Pod*. See if I can figure out what he did wrong."

Leo waited just long enough to get a brief nod of approval from Commander Vasich; then he was gone.

CHAPTER FOUR

Inside *Delta Pod,* the computer replayed Pericles' flight path and then ran through different versions of the same thing. But Leo wasn't watching. He was staring over the top of the monitors and out into the huge, empty blackness of space.

Over his headset, Leo could hear conversations passed along the open lines of the radio channels. He ignored most of it, but a single voice pulled him out of his lonely depression. It was Commander Vasich talking to the rest of the command crew.

"Okay, that's it. We lost him." The were talking about Pericles. They were admitting defeat.

Leo heard Major Santos's voice. "Want to send out another chimp?"

Leo held his breath. Then he heard, "No, it's too dangerous. Shut it down."

The decision happened in a moment. Leo didn't hesitate. He didn't wonder if what he was doing was right or wrong. He just knew he had to do it.

With the press of a button, he sealed the pod's door closed.

· · ·

Up on the flight deck, Hansen the technician watched a light flash on his control board—a light that shouldn't have been flashing at all.

"Um, sir," he said to Commander Vasich. "*Delta Pod*, sir. It's . . . it just launched!"

Vasich used his fist to smash open a radio link on his own command panel. "*Delta Pod*, your flight is not authorized. Repeat, your flight is not authorized!"

"Sorry, Commander," Leo's voice came back over the speaker. "Never send a monkey to do a man's job."

Vasich gritted his teeth. "I swear you'll never fly again!"

"But I sure am flying now!"

The commander's face turned purple with anger. "Alter course. Intercept that pod. No one runs off with one of my—"

"Commander!" Hansen's voice squealed at an alarmingly high pitch. "I think we've got a problem!"

"What?" the commander snapped.

The technician worked his console frantically. "I'm getting a distress signal, sir. It's on our secure channel!"

"Is it *Alpha Pod*?" Major Santos suggested.

Hansen shook his head. "I . . . I don't know. But it's coming on strong."

"Put it up," Vasich said.

The main screen came to life in an explosion of static. Figures jumped in and out of the image, shadowy and undefined. Voices that didn't seem to match the images dropped in and out of the static. ". . . help us . . . massive

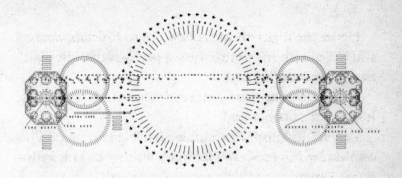

turbulence . . . request instructions . . ." Then it dropped out completely.

"Get it back," Vasich ordered.

"It's gone, sir," the techie replied.

"Jeez," Major Santos whispered.

Vasich lunged for the radio. "*Delta Pod,* abort your mission. Repeat. Abort your mission. Leo!"

Inside *Delta Pod,* Leo heard Vasich's voice, but couldn't make out the words over the interference he was experiencing. The same storm that had interrupted his parents' communication was disrupting the signal between the *Oberon* and *Delta Pod.* But Leo kept right on track, following *Alpha Pod's* course toward the heart of the storm. Among the waves and particles of strange light emanating from the storm, Leo spotted a small white shape. It looked adrift.

Leo activated his microphone. "*Oberon,* I've got a visual on *Alpha Pod,* over."

The only response he got was static.

"*Oberon*, I've got a—"

He stopped, utterly asonished. *Alpha Pod* disappeared. It didn't swerve out of view or speed away. It just wasn't there anymore.

"*Ob . . . Oberon?*" Leo said. His voice cracked a little. He was afraid. "*Oberon*, come back . . ."

Leo felt his own words thrown back in his face as *Delta Pod* lurched violently to one side. He checked his instruments, but they had suddenly gone useless—digital readouts flashed meaningless collections of numbers, alarms blaring for no apparent reason. Suddenly, his monitor was awash in blinding light, and the same light filled the small glass portal.

The screen went black, and all the lights on his control console snuffed themselves out. But the pod cabin was still lit by the mysterious glare from outside—a glare that seemed to come from the electromagnetic storm that engulfed his tiny ship.

Leo brought a fist down like a hammer on the command console. He was dead, hanging like a stone in space. With the power out, his life support was nonexistent. A small craft like *Delta Pod* didn't hold enough air for more than a few minutes on its own, and Leo could already feel the little cockpit air growing stale and warm. He knew from too many training missions that there would be a race between that stuffiness and the sudden chill as the raw coldness of space seeped through the metal hull.

Uselessly, he keyed his microphone again, gasping, "*Oberon . . .* come in, *Oberon . . .*"

His only answer came on the wings of the storm. As Leo felt his lungs struggle for breath, a brilliant pulse burst from the center of the electromagnetic disturbance and raced toward him. It struck the pod and tossed it like a toy boat on a tidal wave. Leo was jerked around, and felt his ribs nearly break as his body slammed against the safety belts. Lights and sounds reappeared inside the pod, and Leo vaguely realized that his power was back on, but he was still out of control. Dials spun madly. The clock on the command console was running at high speed, hours and dates flashing by.

Leo closed his eyes, sure that he was about to be crushed by whatever powerful force was throwing his ship around. But after a moment the violent lurching settled into a steady, almost rhythmic banging. Leo opened his eyes.

His view screen had reactivated itself. On the screen he saw a giant ball of blue and purple. He could hear an eerie whistling sound—a sound he hadn't heard in years, not since his boyhood hanging out at the airstrip, learning to fly in old stunt planes. It was a sound he'd heard once before in a plane that was . . .

Falling, he thought. *I'm falling*. He tried to remember to breathe.

CHAPTER FIVE

The smell of burning plastic and metal filled his nostrils. The pod was dropping through the atmosphere at high speed and had begun to flame like a meteor.

His fingers found the retro rockets, but the shock wave must have blown the wiring, because they were dead. The pod felt like it was shaking apart. Leo gritted his teeth to keep them from rattling out of his head and grabbed the manual control lever, fighting for control of his ship.

On the view screen, the blue-purple haze tore away, revealing a dense blanket of green. But that blanket wasn't going to offer a very soft landing if he didn't do something to slow his descent. Leo pulled back on the flight stick, lifting the pod's nose slightly and letting the rushing air strike more of the pod's surface area. It wouldn't stop the pod, of course, but it would slow it down.

"Come on, come on, catch, you high-tech piece of junk, catch," he muttered.

Finally, he felt the pod bank—not a lot, but some of the downward force shifted forward as the pod caught some air, moving forward ever so slightly. But every inch he moved forward meant he was falling a bit slower, thanks to wind resistance.

He didn't have time to see how much he'd slowed down. In the next instant, the green forest rose up to meet him. The pod tore through a canopy of trees, branches striking it like giants pounding on the hull. Then the pod hit something so hard that it nearly knocked his jaw of its hinges. But the impact wasn't hard enough to be the ground. It had to be . . .

Water started pouring in through cracks in the hull. In seconds Leo was under water. He reached for the hatch release, but it had been melted shut by the fall. He pulled at it frantically, furious that he'd survived a twenty-five-mile fall only to drown in a mud puddle.

At the last minute he remembered the ejection seat. Leo reached for the ejection lever and jerked it hard. A muted roar filled his ears and he was blinded by violent, churning bubbles. Still strapped into the seat, Leo was lifted up and out of the pod like a torpedo. He ripped himself free and followed the bubbles upward. His head broke the surface and he nearly screamed as he sucked in air.

Leo's arms and legs felt like they were made of lead, but he treaded water long enough to catch sight of the shore—then he forced himself to swim for it. It couldn't have been more than ten feet, but it felt like ten miles. Finally, he dragged himself up onto the mud and collapsed.

He snapped out of an unconscious stupor. He didn't

know how long he'd been out. It might have been minutes or hours. The star pilot stood up, wincing. He was a mass of cuts and bruises, his head felt like it had been slammed against a bulkhead, and he had no idea where he was.

How many tree-covered planets are there in this solar system? he wondered.

Did anyone witness his fall through the atmosphere? Would there be a recovery team? Leo had a lot of questions, but no answers. For now, he could only assume he was on his own.

A strangled cry interrupted his thoughts. Instinctively, Leo crouched, hearing something thrash its way through the jungle nearby. Not knowing what else to do, and not wanting to be a part of whatever caused that scream, Leo bolted.

Staying low, he scrambled away from the sounds of approach. But whoever was after him was much faster. Abandoning escape, Leo snatched a rock off the ground and turned to fight.

At the same moment a figure burst through the trees. It was definitely human, but it was like no human Leo had ever seen. The man was half-naked and carried a mesh sack made of vines. It was filled with fruit. By the gray streaks in his tangled hair and beard, Leo guessed that he was in his late forties.

The wild human looked surprised to see him and stopped, staring at him as if Leo were the strange-looking creature.

Leo was about to speak when another human appeared through the bushes. It was a young woman, beautiful beneath a layer of dirt. She stepped forward, slapped the rock from Leo's hand, then turned to the older man. "Father, they're coming. Hurry!"

She bolted off into the woods with the man behind her. Leo, still stunned, watched five or six other humans dash past him. They were all running from something, and Leo decided that he didn't want to know what it was. He took off after the primitive humans, limping on his still-shaking legs.

He continued to hear the sounds of cracking branches and snapping twigs all around him, and at first he assumed it was more humans. But now those sounds were intermingled with the odd hint of metal, like a tinkling of bells. He glanced to either side and behind, and caught a glimpse of dark figures moving through the forest with terrifying speed.

Ignoring his aches, Leo picked up his speed. He ran fast enough to catch up with the slowest of the humans moving ahead of him. Just as he caught sight of the human's back, an enormous shadow dropped out of the trees and smothered the human, who gave out a strangled cry.

More cries filled the jungle. Leo saw something hurtle past him and realized it was a human being that had been tossed into the air. Not far off, he saw a terrified young man suddenly pulled into the underbrush as though the jungle itself had swallowed him. With no more thought than a frightened animal, Leo kept running.

A few paces ahead the trees thinned, and Leo caught sight of an open field. The old man with the fruit bag was already there, as was the girl. Leo sprinted ahead, desperate to get away from whatever terrifying monsters lived in that jungle.

A shadow dropped into his path. Leo froze— and got his first glimpse of one of the creatures that had been chasing him.

It was a gorilla.

Only it couldn't be a gorilla, because it was wearing armor across its massive chest, and its head was covered with a tall helmet. It roared at him and bared its long canines.

Leo felt his heart stop. "Jesus," he whispered.

The gorilla stalked toward him. Leo backed up and tripped over a loose branch. Scrambling to his feet, he snatched up the branch and held it like a spear.

The armored gorilla stared at him quizzically for a moment; then its face twisted into an angry snarl. It rushed forward with blinding speed, snapping the branch in two and lifting Leo clean off his feet. The next thing Leo knew he was flying through the air.

Leo thought he would be dead the next moment, but

the gorilla seemed to have moved on to other targets. The ragged pilot sat up, so stunned by everything that had happened that he no longer felt surprised to see more gorillas—a whole squad of armored primates— melt out of the jungle. Several of them carried weapons called bolas—three weighted balls attached by three ropes. They began to whirl them around their heads. Then they hurled them through the trees toward the humans that had reached the clearing. Each bola found its mark with frightening accuracy, and the humans went down. As if on cue, more gorillas appeared, hefting a large net hemmed with bells. They shook it as they marched forward, frightening the humans.

The net swept over Leo and he rolled away, dropping down into a small ditch.

Leo jumped to his feet and took off in the other direction. He passed a man holding a little girl and watched the man get knocked off his feet. The little girl was snatched away, and the man himself vanished beneath a pile of swarming gorillas.

This can't be happening, Leo thought. *I've gone crazy and I'm seeing things. Or I'm still trapped inside the pod, and I'm actually drowning, and this is a hallucination of some kind.*

Leo saw a young man suddenly lifted up into the trees by gorillas hiding above him. He saw the gray-haired man with the fruit sack get struck across the back and fall to his knees with the beautiful girl beside him.

Leo decided to attack.

An ape on horseback crashed through the forest,

dragging two helpless humans behind it. Gathering his strength, Leo leaped at the horse, grabbing the reins and swinging himself up behind the startled primate. Leo shoved at the gorilla. Even through its armor, Leo could feel how immensely strong the creature was. But the gorilla was so surprised to see a human fight back that it lost its balance and went over the side of the horse.

"Hyah!" Leo said, digging his boots into the horse's side. The horse reared up—and suddenly Leo felt himself rising even higher, right up into the tree branches. A huge hairy face appeared a few inches from his own. Leo realized that a gorilla, holding on to a tree branch with its hands, had plucked him out of the saddle using its feet. The gorilla snarled at him and then let go.

Leo plunged to the ground and hit it sharply. All the air was punched out of his lungs. He looked up to see the face of the gorilla he'd first attacked. The gorilla snorted and raised a foot. Then it stomped down on Leo's head. Everything went dark.

CHAPTER SIX

Attar pushed the helmet back on his head and wiped the damp, matted fur on his forehead. It was a hot day. Sixteen years in the army and he never could get used to the heat.

But he was all gorilla, and a military ape born and bred. No amount of discomfort would make him break with protocol, so he pulled the helmet back down over his thick brow and strapped it into place.

"Report," Attar growled.

A younger gorilla without even a hint of silver on his back lifted a small piece of parchment. "The final count's not done yet, sir, but we've trapped enough humans to fill a dozen carts."

Attar nodded approvingly as he watched his apes work. They were busy trussing up the last of the humans and tossing them into cages on the backs of the carts. Attar's sharp eyes caught sight of the human woman who'd nearly gotten away, along with her sire, the old one who'd stolen the fruit. Attar noted that the old human sported a number of bruises. Even though Attar was just following orders, he never felt a lack of job satisfaction. He knew that humans were wild and dangerous animals, and they had to be kept in their place no matter what it took.

Then Attar spotted the young human male, the one who had pushed one of his soldiers off his horse and had dared shake a stick at Attar himself. The human was half-conscious, his arms strapped behind his back as he waited to be loaded into a cart. Attar felt his anger rise. He trotted over to the cage where the human lay. Like all humans, this one was nearly bald. It made him think of worms. The creature's eyes fluttered. Attar wished the human were awake so he could torment it. Well, perhaps he could shake it awake, Attar thought.

The gorilla raised his fist, but at that moment a trumpet sounded.

Leo Davidson hovered between wakefulness and sleep. He kept seeing flashes of light from the electromagnetic storm cloud. But there were figures scurrying about in the light—gigantic hair-covered figures encased in armor. Suddenly, one of the figures appeared right before him. It opened its mouth, revealing sharp fangs. When it roared, the sound that burst from its throat was like a loud, angry trumpet.

Leo woke with a start, but the world he woke into was worse than his nightmare. He was lying facedown in the dirt, his arms tied behind his back. Other bodies were pressed against him on either side, and he heard moans and whimpers. Slowly, he rolled onto his back and sat up, blinking in the sunlight. Around him he could see carts bearing huge cages, and inside the cages, human beings had been packed like sardines. Gorillas moved among the cages, checking locks, harnessing horses, and sometimes rattling the cages to scare the humans packed inside.

Unsteadily, Leo climbed to his feet, but just as he did, all the humans around him seemed to cower and look down. At the same time, the gorillas all snapped to attention.

Riding through the midst of the scene, his entrance announced by the sound of the trumpets, was a huge gorilla wearing a gold uniform. He rode on the back of an enormous black stallion, and he glared down at both humans and gorillas like a jungle king. Leo was fascinated. The big ape carried himself like a lord.

Leo was so intrigued by the gorilla that he didn't realize he was the only human staring right at the creature. The gold-gowned ape turned and met his gaze, then wrinkled his lip. Faster than lightning, the gorilla leaped from his saddle and sprang at Leo, grabbing him by the hair.

"Attar, this one looked at me!" the gorilla said.

Leo was amazed. Words had come out of the gorilla's mouth. Words. It had talked.

The armored gorilla, who must have been called Attar, growled, "He won't do it again."

Leo grabbed the gorilla by the wrist. "You . . . you talk!"

"Take your stinking hands off me, you dirty human!" the gorilla snarled. He backfisted Leo, and the world went dark again.

It might have been the smell of human sweat, or the sound of creaking wheels, or the bump of the carts on the road that woke Leo up. Or it might have been all three. Whatever it was, Leo woke up miserable, lying under the legs of a half-naked and sweaty man with hair covering most of his body.

Leo shoved the man's legs away and sat up with a groan. His stomach felt queasy, and he fought the urge to be sick. He pushed aside the legs of the man lying on top of him. The man grunted at Leo but said nothing in response to Leo's glare.

Leo sat up and looked around. He was in one of the cages atop a cart. There must have been at least twenty humans stuffed into the cage with him like cattle. There were two gorillas sitting at the driver's bench. Leo nearly gagged as he realized what was pulling the cart. There was a team of human men chained to the cart's pull bar. The men wore blinders.

Wordlessly, Leo looked up the road, where it wound its way along the slope of a hill to a walled city in the distance. It was a primitive city made of stone and clay, but it looked well organized. It reminded Leo of ancient cities he'd seen on earth that were built thousands of years ago.

Leo grabbed the bars of the cage and dragged himself onto his feet, staring at the city as they passed beneath a great stone gate. Gorillas, orangutans, chimpanzees, and other simians were everywhere. Gorillas dressed in elegant flowing robes, orangutans dressed in short, workmanlike leather tunics, young apes squealing at each other and dodging in and out of the crowds of adult gorillas passing along the streets, each with his own business in mind. Outside what looked like a café, a group of chimpanzees with gray hair on their heads and backs sat huddled over some kind of board game, squabbling about the positions of certain pieces as they sucked at pipes and blew smoke rings. Beyond them, three female chimps haggled with a fruit vendor over the price of mangoes. An ape street performer had

managed to attract a small crowd with an impressive juggling act in which he used both his hands and his feet. Sitting on a wall, a teenage ape practiced on a flute. The melody he played seemed hauntingly familiar to Leo, but it was gone before he could place it.

And everywhere were humans, too. But not walking free among the great apes. There were humans on the street in the same way you might have seen dogs in the alleys of big cities. The humans in this city of the apes were treated like work animals, beasts of burden. Some were loaded down with packages, walking behind their ape owners. Some pulled carts.

Leo thought he was going to faint. It was real. He could smell it, touch it, hear it—the world around him was *real*.

The reality of his situation struck him in the head in the form of a small, sharp rock. A group of young male gorillas appeared, running alongside the carts and pelting the prisoners with rocks and dirt clods, jeering and teasing the humans inside. Most of the humans cowered, throwing their hands over the heads. Leo stubbornly stood tall, dodging away from any rocks that came near him.

In this way, he was able to see when a female chimpanzee, much older than the children but still young, rushed toward the hooligans.

"Stop it!" she called out. "Stop it! You're being cruel." She grabbed one young ape by the shoulder and shook him. "You. Open your hand. Open it!"

The ape child scowled and reluctantly uncurled his fingers. A stone dropped to the ground.

"Who told you you could throw stones at humans?" the chimp female demanded.

"My father," the adolescent gorilla stated defiantly.

"Then you're both wrong," the female snapped. "And you can tell him I said so. Now go on. Get away from here!"

The ape children sulked and moved off. One of them

paused a moment to look over his shoulder and shout, "Human lover!" before they all chittered and ran off.

The cart passed by, but Leo pushed himself toward the back to catch snatches of the female ape's conversations with another female who came trotting up to her.

"Do you always have to be so intense?" the gorilla female asked. "I thought we were going shopping."

The female who'd stopped the boys didn't answer. She was still staring at the caged humans, and Leo, staring back, caught her eyes. He felt her stare right into him, and the sensation was disturbing. Hers were the first kind eyes he'd seen all day. They looked human and full of clear thoughts . . . but they stared out of the face of an ape.

CHAPTER SEVEN

The carts veered toward the side of the road and pulled to a stop. As they did, Leo could see a procession of gorillas in long red robes stepping solemnly down the street, their faces masked by scarves. They were chanting something low and slow. It was clear to Leo that, gorillas or not, these were obviously monks, and what they were chanting was a prayer.

Attar, the lead gorilla, stepped out of his place at the head of the cart line and stopped before the line of monks. Attar bent his knee and lowered his head. The monks stopped, and the first in line touched his paw to the big gorilla's head, muttering another prayer. By his closed eyes and trembling face, Leo could see that Attar was a spiritual ape.

Leo felt someone pull on his arm, and he was dragged down to his knees. He spun around angrily and found himself looking at the face of a human boy, a teenager. Leo recognized him as the same boy who'd been pulled up into the trees. His hair was wild. His skin was mud-covered and marked with cuts and scrapes. But the eyes that stared out of his filthy face were intelligent and sharp.

"Where am I?" Leo whispered.

The boy shook his head in warning.

Next to the boy huddled the attractive woman Leo had seen earlier, and the old man who'd carried the fruit sack. Leo looked at the woman and said, pleadingly, "What is this place?

The woman hissed a warning and glared at him from under her tangled brown hair.

Leo opened his mouth again to speak, but the old man reached out and grabbed the space pilot under his arm, pinching the skin hard. The man said in a throaty whisper, "The boy is Birn. My name is Karubi. Head down. Mouth shut. You'll get us all killed."

Leo opened his mouth again and the man pinched hard again, bringing tears to the newcomer's eyes.

"Head down. Mouth shut," the man repeated.

Leo nodded. Whatever else this wild human was, he was obviously intelligent. If he was afraid for his life, Leo thought he should probably be, too. He quieted down.

The carts passed under a great stone arch and into an enormous square. High stone walls surrounded the town center on every side. In moments the carts had assembled in the middle of the square, the cages were thrown open, and armored gorillas with whips were driving the humans out into the open. Taking cues from the three humans who had warned him, Leo obeyed every order.

A side door opened and a figure stepped out. It was dressed in blue robes. It threw back its hood, yawned, and stretched in the sunlight, scratching its behind lazily as it finally focused on the humans. It was an orangutan, his orange hair puffed and frazzled at the edges of his face. The orangutan yawned again and pulled a small black cudgel from his robe. Then he shook his head and started forward.

The orangutan, in no hurry, made one entire circle around the mob of filthy humans before he finally grunted and approached one of the soldier apes.

"Are you trying to put me out of business?" the orangutan complained. His voice was carefully measured. "These are the skankiest, scabbiest, scuzziest humans I've ever seen."

The soldier would have none of it. "You don't want them, Limbo?" he said gruffly.

The orangutan, Limbo, scratched his head. "Hmm-mph. I'll take the whole lot. I'll have to make it up on volume."

Limbo whistled, and a squad of apes wearing sanitation masks hustled out of the door and over to the humans. As Limbo paid the soldier, the masked apes began to separate the humans into groups. Leo saw Karubi bend his head low and whisper to the woman, "Daena, don't be afraid."

"I'll find you!" she whispered back.

Suddenly Limbo himself appeared between them. He sneered. "Very touching. Really. I can't see for the tears in my eyes. Now move!" The orangutan snatched a handful of Daena's hair and dragged her out of the crowd. "To the female pen!"

"Daena!" Karubi yelled, trying to reach the woman, who was obviously his daughter. A handler struck his outstretched arm with a cudgel, and the old man yelped.

Leo felt himself grabbed by powerful hands and thrown into a pen with most of the other men. The boy, Birn, was dragged that way, too, but there was a brief pause as he struggled. An ape put a hand too close to his mouth, and Birn bit down hard. The ape shrieked, but the boy didn't let go even when the ape tried to shake him off.

Calmly, Limbo strode forward and grabbed Birn by the hair. He punched the boy in the throat and Birn let go, choking. Limbo threw him into the pen and turned to his handler, clicking his tongue. "How many times do I have to tell you? Wear your gloves when you handle humans."

"Are you going soft, Limbo?"

The voice belonged to Thade, the lead gorilla, with

Attar at his side. Limbo whirled around, the arrogant look on his furry face morphing into a wheedling smile. "General Thade, what a pleasant surprise. And an honor, of course, to have you at my establishment."

Thade pointed to Birn, who was being helped to his feet by the other humans. "You used to hack off a limb when they caused too much trouble."

Limbo nodded. "Yes, of course, sir, but those were better times. These days, unfortunately, I need all the money I can wring out of them, and the creature is worth a lot less if he's been damaged."

Attar brushed past Limbo and approached the pen. The gorilla commander eyed Leo threateningly. "Don't turn your back on this one. He's feisty."

Limbo chuckled. "Were these the ones raiding the orchards, sir? I know an old country remedy that never fails. Gut one and string the carcass up—"

Thade silenced him with a wave of his paw. "The human rights faction is already nipping at my heels."

Limbo snorted. "Do-gooders. Who needs them? I'm all for free speech—as long as they keep their mouths shut."

Thade strolled over to a pen where the children had been separated and eyed them carefully. "I promised my niece a pet for her birthday."

Limbo hunched his shoulders, looking even readier to please. "Ah, excellent, sir! The little ones make wonderful pets . . . but make sure you get rid of it by puberty. If there's one thing you don't want in your house it's a human teenager."

Out from the ranks of ape soldiers, a female gorilla and a youngster appeared, following in Thade's footsteps. "Do you see anything you like, niece?" General Thade asked.

"Anything at all!" Limbo piped up. "It's yours!"

The young ape eyed the human children in the pen like a human looking at puppies in a pet store. Finally, she shyly pointed to a human girl about five years old.

"Excellent choice!" Limbo applauded.

Attar opened the cage and snatched the girl, who squealed. From his own pen, Leo kept his eyes on Daena. Beneath her matted hair, her eyes burned into the gorillas.

Thade made sure his relatives were a safe distance from the filthy pens and then leaped easily onto his horse.

Limbo, still trying to make an impression, said, "Ah, uh, General, they say if you piss along the fence line it keeps them away from the crops."

Thade curled his lip. "Stay back, Limbo. You stink of humans."

Leo watched the general whirl his horse around and ride away.

CHAPTER EIGHT

Leo had commanded himself to relax, and, following the example of the other humans, to submit to the apes.

All that ended when the branding irons came out. The gorillas began to stoke fires, and to heat metal bars inside those fires. When the irons were white hot, they began to tether humans one by one, drag them out of the pens, and tie them to posts set into the ground of the square.

Leo watched in horror as Daena was caught by a noose around her neck and hauled out of the female pen. The rags were torn from her shoulders, and one of the gorillas pressed a hot iron to her shoulder blade. Daena winced and bit her lip, tears welling in her eyes. But she didn't make a sound. The iron hissed as it burned her skin. Then the gorillas were done. They threw her back into the pen and moved on.

Two of the handlers opened the male cage and set their eyes on Leo. Before he could react, they had grabbed hold of his arms. He dug his heels into the ground but the two strong gorillas easily overpowered him and dragged him to the branding post.

Desperately, Leo kicked and squirmed. He managed to release the grip of one of the two apes, then twisted himself away from the other.

Limbo groaned. "Do I have to do everything myself?" He snatched up a branding iron and stalked toward Leo menacingly.

"Limbo, stop!"

The trader turned to see a female chimpanzee scowling at him. Leo risked a glance at her and recognized the same female that had stopped the boys from throwing rocks. Now she strode forward arrogantly and grabbed the branding iron from Limbo's hand. She tossed it into the mud.

Limbo slapped one long-fingered paw against his forehead. "By Semos, not you again!"

The female stiffened. "I will not stand idly by while humans are being mistreated and tortured—"

"Ari!" Limbo interrupted hotly. "The only reason I put up with your nonsense is because of your father. But you test my patience!"

The female, Ari, shrugged. "If you want me to stop harassing you, then give up your bloody business."

Limbo opened his hands wide, his long, delicate fingers facing up to the sky. The handlers set to watch Leo trained their gaze on the drama unfolding between the two apes. Leo seized his opportunity. He glanced around, looking for a weapon, and spotted a length of chain half-buried in the mud.

Limbo said, "Hey, I do the job nobody else wants. I don't see any of you bleeding hearts spending all day with these dangerous, dirty, dumb beasts—"

"They are not dumb!" Ari said, stamping her foot. "They can be taught to live with us, and I'm going to prove it!"

Quick as he could manage, Leo reached down and grabbed the chain. He whipped it around the nearest handler's foot and yanked. The gorilla yelped and fell off balance, his spear popping into the air. In one smooth motion Leo snatched it and leaned forward and touched the end of the spear to Ari's neck. She gasped.

Limbo, calm and unconcerned, laughed out loud. "There's your proof! Now I'll have to put this one down!"

Leo wrapped one hand around Ari's neck and used the other to press the spear point against her throat. Instantly they were surrounded by handlers.

He looked at Ari, who was staring at him with a mixture of surprise and fear. But instead of threatening her, he leaned in close and whispered desperately, "Please . . . help me."

This seemed to startle the female even more.

"Watch it!" one of the handlers yelled.

All eyes followed the warning. As Leo held everyone's attention, Daena had realized that the female pen was open. She made a break for freedom. Limbo sprinted after her and stunned her with one blow, knocking her to the ground. Obviously irritated now, he turned back and stalked toward Ari. "Look what you've started! Now I'm getting a headache!"

He came closer and Leo hunched down, pressing the spear blade against Ari's throat until it nearly punctured the skin.

"Oh, please!" Limbo said, raising his hands in surrender. "Don't hurt her!" He took another step forward, keeping his hands well within view. Leo watched him suspiciously, making sure those hands were well out of reach.

And suddenly the spear was gone, snatched from his hand.

By the orangutan's foot.

Limbo had used his nimble foot to grab the spear away. Without warning he brought the dull handle crashing down on Leo's head. Stunned, Leo collapsed into the mud with Limbo standing over him.

"Who needs this aggravation," the trader growled. He motioned to several of his handlers, who shuffled forward. "Hold him."

As the handlers pinned Leo's arms and legs against the ground, the trader reversed the spear and raised it, ready to plunge the sharp tip into Leo's body.

"Wait!" Ari yelled. Limbo paused.

"Sell him to me."

The trader gasped. "What? Are you crazy? He's wild—" He motioned to Daena. "They're both wild!"

Ari straightened up, stiffening her resolve. "Then I'll buy them both."

Leo recognized the sound of greed in the trader's voice. "Buy them, eh? That would be expensive. *Very* expensive."

Ari said, "I'm sure we could come to a deal."

Limbo chuckled. "I'm sure we could."

Leo felt the paws that held him relax. He knew now that he wasn't going to be killed. He heard Ari say, "Deliver them to my house."

"Certainly," Limbo said. "I just have to mark him first."

Before Leo realized what that meant, he felt hot iron press into his flesh. He let out a scream of pure agony.

He had just been branded.

CHAPTER NINE

There were times, Ari had to admit, when she doubted her resolve.

It wasn't easy being one of the few apes in the entire city who believed in human rights.

She was constantly teased and taunted by acquaintances. Most of her friends, and even her own family, felt awkward around her. They didn't know how to act naturally, always afraid she was going to scold them for mistreating their humans.

But she couldn't help it, she admitted as she walked home that evening. Something in her wouldn't let her believe that humans were mere animals. She believed it right down to the core of her apehood. And as dangerous as that human was, he had proved it by the way he had looked at her. A part of Ari was furious that he had threatened her, but the stronger part of her knew that he had been terrified and desperate.

It was by thinking of that desperate human that she managed to maintain her composure while her father ranted and raved at her that evening.

"You did *what!?*" he shouted as soon as he'd heard. His

name was Sandar, and he was one of the most important apes in the entire community. His handsome face and back were marked by distinguished silver streaks. He had been a member of the senate for decades, and every ape who knew him was proud to call him friend. He had a reputation for diplomacy, always finding common ground when politics became too hostile.

But all that had been thrown out the window now. He was now just an angry father who'd heard that his daughter had been in danger.

"I forbid, I absolutely forbid you to carry on this nonsense if you insist on putting your life in jeopardy!" Sandar said, slapping his open palm on the kitchen table.

Instinctively, another ape in the room took a step forward. This was Krull, a hulking elderly gorilla, a silverback past his prime but still incredibly strong. He had been in Sandar's service for years, and now he watched over Ari. When they argued this way, as they did so often of late, Krull felt his loyalty pulled in two directions.

"Father," Ari said soothingly. "I promise. I couldn't hold myself back when I saw how those poor creatures were being treated. But I know it was dangerous. I won't do it again."

Sandar opened his mouth to snap back. He flexed his jaw for a moment, revealing his canines; then his lips zipped shut. "Very well," he said, clearing his throat. "Thank you. But there is still the matter of these humans."

Sandar waved a paw at four humans kneeling on the

kitchen floor. Two of them were his own house humans, Tival and Bon. They were well groomed and well trained, as much a part of his estate as his horse and carriage. But beside them knelt two savage beasts—barely clothed and probably full of lice and fleas.

"Father," Ari said, maintaining a calm and reassuring voice. "Please. I'll pay for them with my own money."

Sandar groaned. "Your 'own money' is going to make a pauper out of me. What are we going to do with them?" He strode over to the humans, careful not to get too near. Tival and Bon instantly leaped to their feet.

Krull, the bodyguard, lumbered forward. "Rise when your master addresses you!" he growled.

Daena scowled at the silverback. Krull clutched at her hand and pulled her to her feet with no effort. Leo gulped and rose slowly, facing Sandar.

Sandar sighed and shook his head. "Semos help me. Wild humans in my house."

Ari pointed at Leo. "This one is different."

Sandar scoffed. "How different can they be? You can't tell one from another."

The sound of a bell trilled down the corridors. "My guests are here," Sandar said. He cast a warning glance at his daughter. "Ari, I want you to be on your best behavior. Keep those savages out of their sight . . . especially away from General Thade."

"Father . . . ," Ari began. She did not appreciate General Thade's unwanted attentions.

"And you'd better be nice to him!"

• • •

Ari sat at the table with her friend Leeta as her father greeted his guests. He welcomed each one as though he or she were the reason for his dinner party.

Ari herself disliked almost everyone who walked through the door, and she would have a hard time hiding it.

There was Senator Nado, an old orangutan with a round belly and a pompous look on his face. Beside him was his (very young) wife, Nova.

"Good evening, Senator Nado," Sandar said, touching his face to the other ape's gently. "And my dear Nova, you do look lovely tonight."

The young chimp, Nova, stroked the fur on her face self-consciously. "I'm having a bad hair day."

Senator Nado rolled his eyes. "Yet she spends a fortune grooming herself."

Nova purred, "And I'm worth every penny."

They glided toward the dinner table.

At the table, Leeta leaned close to Ari and said, "The general will be here soon. He's powerful and aggressive. What else could you want in a male?"

Ari said simply, "Someone I can respect . . . and who respects me."

Leeta shook her head disapprovingly. "Don't play so hard to get. Say yes to him, and you'll be invited to every exclusive party in the city."

"Oh, please, Leeta, how many silly parties can you go to?"

Leeta brushed back her hair and smiled coyly. "How many are there?"

Ari would have responded, but her father had gathered up his guests and was guiding them to the table, and it was time for proper greetings. She took a deep breath.

In the kitchen, the sound of a ringing bell signaled that the guests had been seated. Instantly, Tival and Bon, the house humans, leaped to their feet. They grabbed wooden trays of food from the counter and hurried to the stairs that led up to the dining hall.

As soon as they were gone, Leo, too, jumped to his feet—and headed right for the kitchen window. It was covered by wooden shutters. When he tried to move them, they wouldn't budge.

He turned and looked at Daena. Now that they were alone, the question that had been welling up inside him finally came out. "How did these monkeys get this way!?" he demanded.

Daena looked at him as though he were insane. "What other way would they be?"

Leo shook his head. "They'd be begging me for a treat."

Daena eyed him carefully. She'd never met a human

like him before. He reminded her more of a gorilla: proud, impatient, sure of himself. "What tribe are you from?"

"It's called the United States Air Force. And I'm going back to it."

Suddenly, the big gorilla Krull appeared. Leo had the sense that Krull was sharp despite his silence and his hulking presence. He had the eyes of a drill sergeant.

"No talk," Krull growled. "Finish your work." He lifted another plate of food and walked back up the stairs.

Leo looked around for another avenue of escape and saw a doorway, but it was tightly locked. With nothing else to do, he picked up a tray and tiptoed to the top of the stairs. He listened to the apes' conversation.

"You know, we just returned from a trip to our country house in the rain forest."

"And how was it?" Sandar asked politely.

"Boring," Nova intoned.

Nado leaned back in his chair. "I find it relaxing . . . being away from the frantic pace of the city."

Nova put on a face that seemed burdened with too many cares. "I wanted to go out. But there was no place to go . . . nothing but trees and rocks." She slapped her husband lightly on the hand. "All you did was nap."

The old senator nodded. "Exactly. A bit of time away from politics is what is needed for a weary soul like me."

Ari leaned over to Leeta and whispered something out of earshot of her guests, but within Leo's hearing. "Look at the old fool. He left his wife and children for her, a chimp half his age. Now he can't keep up."

Leeta raised an eyebrow knowingly. "But he's worth a fortune."

Nado nudged Sandar. "We used to lose ourselves for days in the forest when were young, didn't we, Sandar? Now I can barely climb a tree."

Ari's father nodded. "It's trite but true. Youth is wasted on the young. Now that I have so much to do, I find myself exhausted. Still, some nights I dream of hurtling through the branches." Sandar sighed. "How did I get so old so fast?"

"Living with your daughter would age any ape quickly."

It was the second time that voice had announced the entrance of the most powerful ape in the city. No one rose, but everyone seemed to snap to attention as General Thade strode in, an impressive figure whose presence barely seemed to fit inside the dining room. Behind him, Attar stood in attendance.

"Quick, switch seats with me," Ari whispered.

Leeta refused to move. "He's here to see *you*."

Thade strode forward toward the empty chair next to Ari and waited for Krull to pull it out. Leo was surprised to see that Krull, who had been so attentive before, now stood stock-still. After an awkward moment, Attar jumped forward, pulled the chair out, and then slid it back in as General Thade sat down. Thade locked eyes with Krull, and Leo thought he could have drawn a line of fire between them.

"General Thade," Sandar said, raising a glass, "you are too long a stranger in our house."

Thade bowed his head in acknowledgement of the toast. "My apologies, senator. I stopped to see my father."

"How is my old friend doing?" Ari's father asked.

Thade allowed himself a deep sigh. "I'm afraid he's slipping. I wish I could spend more time with him . . . but these are troubled times. Humans infest the provinces —"

"Because our cities encroach on their habitat," Ari blurted automatically.

Thade kept his eyes on Sandar, refusing to look at Ari. "They breed quickly while we grow soft with our affluence. Even now they outnumber us ten to one."

Nova picked at a bowl of grapes. "Why can't the government simply sterilize them all?"

Her husband, Senator Nado, shook his head. "The cost would be prohibitive . . . although our scientists do tell me the humans carry terrible diseases."

Ari objected. "How would we know? The army burns the bodies before they can be examined." She turned to Sandar for back up. "Father?"

Sandar wriggled in his chair, uncomfortable at being trapped by his daughter's uncontrollable enthusiasm. "Well, at times, perhaps, the senate has felt that the army has been a tad . . . extreme."

Thade shrugged off the comment. "Extremism in the defense of apes is no vice."

Tival and Bon entered with the main course and hurriedly set dishes down in front of each ape at the table. Senator Nado reached hungrily for a piece of fruit and was about to bite into it when Attar uttered a low, cautionary growl. The senator rolled his eyes, but all the others seemed willing to go along with Attar, so he dropped the fruit and bowed his head. They all lowered their faces, and Attar began to pray.

"We give thanks to you, Semos, for the fruit of the land. Bless us, Holy Father, who created all apes in his image. Hasten the Day when you will return . . . and bring peace to your children. Amen."

"Amen," the others repeated.

At the top of the stairs, Leo shook his head. He had a moment to reflect—rare since he'd crash-landed in this strange place and been enslaved. This world was like a parallel universe, like a more primitive Earth, but where apes had become the dominant species and humans were merely animals, living in the wild. The apes had their own cities, and they even had a religion of some kind. What had happened to him inside that storm?

Leo heard some apes come through the locked door. He hefted his tray and started out into the dining room, pretending to serve but hoping to catch some important bit of information. As Leo approached, Thade sniffed, wrinkling his nose in disgust. He turned to face Leo for a moment and then looked at Sandar.

"What is this beast doing in your house?" the general demanded.

Sandar looked directly at his daughter, demanding that she take responsibility for this.

Ari hesitated a moment and then stated, "He'll be trained as a domestic."

Thade broke the silence that followed Ari's controversial statement. "Your ideas threaten our prosperity. The human problem will not be solved by throwing money at it. The government tried once, and all we got was a welfare state that nearly bankrupted us."

Attar sniffed the air unpleasantly. "And changed the face of the city."

Leeta agreed. "I think the city has about as much diversity as it can handle."

Ari spared a cold, unfriendly glance toward her friend. Then, carefully, she withdrew a small embroidered scarf from her gown. It was simple, but carefully sewn. "This," she said triumphantly, "was made by one of my humans. Can you deny its skill? Isn't it obvious that they are capable of real culture?"

Thade snorted. "Everything in 'human culture' takes place below the waist."

The other guests laughed at his off-color joke.

Senator Nado added, "Really, my dear, next you'll be telling me that these creatures have souls."

Ari said matter-of-factly, "Of course they do."

Across the table, Attar stiffened. His religious sensibilities had been offended. "The senator's daughter," he warned, "flirts with blasphemy."

While all this had gone on, Leo had been standing still. His only goal now was to keep as quiet as possible, and to make as little trouble as possible, so that they'd leave him alone until he could escape. And if that meant suffering under Thade's comments, he'd force himself to do it.

Even as he thought that, Thade grabbed him by the arm and pulled Leo's face within inches of his own. As Leo's tray of food went flying, Thade pried Leo's mouth open and peered down his tightening throat.

"Is there a soul in you?" Thade scoffed. He threw Leo to the ground roughly, and the other apes joined Thade's crude laughter.

Leo felt heat and anger rise up in him, but he ignored them. Instead, he began to pick up the scraps of food he'd spilled.

A small smile crossed Leo's face. As he picked up the contents of the tray, he found a small, sharp implement, like a fork, that the apes used for eating. He slipped it into the sleeve of his shirt.

Now he had a weapon.

CHAPTER TEN

Ari jumped to her feet, her chair clattering to the floor behind her. "You are all cruel and petty. I've lost my appetite."

She stormed up to her room, trying hard not to look like a pouting child. The room was dark, but she found a match and, by memory, she walked over to a candle and lit it. Instantly a sweet odor filled the air. Light from the candle fell on the image of a blissful ape. The ape smiled at her as though she had nothing to worry about in the world.

"Undoubtedly, you are praying to Semos for patience."

Ari whirled around. General Thade stood in the doorway remarkably silent. "You have a habit of sneaking up on people, General," she said stiffly.

"I never took you for the religious type." He pointed to the candle and the image of Semos, the messiah who had brought salvation to the apes. And, if you believed the monks, Semos would return some day to lead the apes to paradise.

Thade made his way casually into the room. Ari said

coldly, "And I never took you for the type to mistreat helpless ani—" She stopped herself.

"Helpless animals?" he said with a wide-faced grin. "Exactly. They are animals, Ari. Argue for the better treatment of *animals,* and you might bend an ear or two. But argue for making them more than animals, and you'll just wear out your voice."

He reached the candle and held his paw up to the flame. Finally, he said, "I have no patience for these society dinners. I only came here to see you."

Ari felt her mouth go dry. "Then you've wasted your time."

Smoothly, his hand went from the candle to her neck, caressing it, and holding it, too, so she couldn't back away.

"My feelings haven't changed since the last time we spoke," he said softly. "You know how much I care for you."

"You only care about my father's influence. And your own ambition," she added.

She turned her head as he tried to nuzzle her and managed to pull away from him. He reached after her, but his hand clutched only the scarf made by humans.

Thade curled his lip, showing his canines. His voice changed in an instant. The soft-spoken lover was gone, replaced by a general hardened by war. "I know about the trouble you caused today. I could have you arrested."

But Ari now could see him for what he was. A petty, jilted ape.

"What I did was right," she said firmly. "I'd do it again."

Thade shook his head and backed away, his canines still long and bare in his mouth. When he reached the door, he said simply, "You feel so much for the humans . . . yet you can't feel anything for me."

He said the word *humans* like a curse. Then he was gone.

General Thade left Sandar's house without saying good-bye. His long, strong fingers swam through the scarf as he pondered this young female. She was right, of course. He wanted her for her father's influence. A general with such a strong ally in the senate could do almost anything. But he did also care for her, in his own way.

Thade reached his horse and barely acknowledged Attar as he leaped onto its back.

"Sir," his aide said. "A moment, please."

Thade looked at him darkly. "What is it?"

Two soldiers melted out of the darkness and stood at attention, their backs straight.

"What?" he demanded.

Attar said, "These apes insist on speaking to you, sir. They won't tell me what it's about, but they insist it's urgent."

Thade ordered the two apes to speak. As he listened, his eyes opened wide in surprise.

● ● ●

The two soldiers led the general and Attar through the forests east of the city. It was land Thade knew well—he had been there earlier that same day, driving humans from the orchards. The creatures infested the fruit groves like fleas on a dog.

Beyond the groves lay an immense bog. Humans didn't go there because of mosquitoes. Apes didn't go there simply because there was nothing to be had there. The soldiers had been stationed merely to watch for stray humans who might wander that way from the orchards.

When the soldiers signaled a halt, Thade dismounted quickly. He walked to the edge. Now and then something disturbed the water—a fish, or a frog—and the dark surface rippled.

Thade said curtly, "Tell me again."

The two ape soldiers trotted forward.

"Something fell out of the sky," the first began.

"With wings of fire," the second said. "And it was screaming."

"Semos." Attar, a few paces back and holding the reins of the horses, had let the word slip.

Thade smiled to himself. He was surprised Attar had held the word in so long. For all his skill at warcraft, Attar was a simple ape. He cared about two things only: following his god and following orders. That's what made him such a good soldier.

But these others, Thade wasn't so sure about. "Are you sure you didn't dream this?" he demanded.

"No, sir!" one of the two answered quickly. "Look!" He pointed to a line of trees. In the moonlight, they stuck up like jagged, broken teeth. Something had torn through them with great violence.

"Where is it now?" Thade asked.

"It splashed down in there," the first went on, pointing out into the darkness. "But not far from the shore."

Thade put his paws at his waist, adjusting the heft of his belt. His paw passed over the hilt of a knife. "Who else have you told?"

The first ape straightened up. "No one, sir. We knew we had to come right to you."

Thade grinned. "You did exactly the right thing."

CHAPTER ELEVEN

Clang!

The cage door slammed shut and Krull locked it.

Without so much as a good night, he turned and shuffled off, dousing the lights and leaving the humans alone, caged in a corner of the darkened kitchen.

The two human slaves, Tival and Bon, instantly curled up in separate corners and fell asleep. Leo waited for a while, listening for any sounds from beyond the kitchen. Daena said nothing.

When time had passed, Leo slipped the sharp prong out of his sleeve and reached through the bars of the cage. The *tink-tink* sound of the prong scraping against the lock sounded loud in his ears, but he was sure it didn't carry out of the kitchen.

"What are you doing?" Daena whispered hoarsely.

"Enjoying the benefits of a misspent youth," he replied.

"What?"

"I'm picking the lock," he explained, just as the lock popped open.

The sound of the cage door opening was quieter even than Daena's whisper, but Tival and Bon jumped up as though an explosion had just rocked their world. They stared at Leo, then at the open cage, then back to Leo. Bon simply said, "There's a curfew for humans."

Tival nodded, unable to take his eyes off the open cage. "If you're found on the street at night . . . they'll kill you on sight."

Leo pointed to the bars of the cage. "And if you stay here you're already dead."

He stepped out of the cage and Daena followed him eagerly. They turned and looked at the two house slaves. Tival hesitated, then stepped out of the cage.

All three escapees looked back at Bon. But Bon only stepped backward, pressing herself against the inside of the cage. "Our mistress has been so kind to us," she said.

Daena frowned. "She's your enemy."

Leo waited one second longer and then turned away. He didn't have time to deal with people who didn't want their freedom.

He hurried through the dark kitchen to a drawer and found a knife. He stashed it in his robe and turned to Daena.

"Can you lead me back to the place where they caught us?"

Daena nodded. Leo hurried toward the door, but the girl hadn't moved.

"Not without my father," she said simply.

Leo grimaced. His quick escape was about to turn into a rescue mission. "It's too dangerous," he argued. "We have to go right now."

"Then you can look for the place on your own."

Leo bit his lip. "Look, you don't have a clue who I am. Or where I'm from. And you wouldn't understand if I told you. But I can help you."

Daena nodded and then said, "And you can start by helping me find my father."

Limbo's quandrangle at night was a quiet place.

He liked it that way. The truth was, Limbo was a peaceful ape at heart. He liked his quiet, and he liked to be clean, and he had precious few opportunities for either one in his business. Late at night, he liked to retreat to the solitude of his own chambers at the top of his house and pamper himself.

That night, he'd chosen orange blossoms. He crushed them in a stone bowl and then, standing in front of a mirror, he began to rub them over his arms and legs. Tomorrow, the stink of humans would cover him again. But at least for tonight he could relax.

If Limbo had stared in the other direction out into the courtyard, he might have seen three shadows hurry across the muddy square to the human pens.

Daena and Leo took the lead, with Tival following nervously behind. They'd made their way quietly and quickly across the city. Sneaking through the streets had been easier than they thought. All they had to do was stay quiet and out of sight.

Daena crouched down beside the gate to the human pen and peeked between the slates. She nearly jumped back when a pair of eyes met hers, reflected by the moonlight. It was Karubi, as alert as ever.

"How did you—?" he began to ask.

"Later, Father," she interrupted. "Take this rope. Pass it back through."

Leo formed a makeshift vise around the middle slat of the cage. He crushed the slat until it snapped with a loud crunch.

Everyone froze, listening. But no one came.

The gate to the slave pen rattled loose. The old man Karubi stepped out, followed by the wild-looking boy named Birn, and a third young man Daena called Gunnar.

Daena's eyes went immediately to Karubi's arm, which was bent stiffly at the elbow and pressed against his ribs. "You're hurt," she said.

He ignored his arm and her comment and hugged her. "How did you get away?"

Daena motioned to Leo. Karubi appraised the other human slowly. "Who are you?"

Leo shrugged. "Just somebody trying to get the hell out of here."

Gunnar eyed Tival, who kept looking around nervously. Gunnar growled. "This is one of their house humans. He thinks he's better than us . . . he thinks he's part ape."

Leo groaned. He had no time for this. To Daena, he said, "You promised to show me the way back."

"We'll go together," Karubi said quickly.

A few moments later the shadows, now doubled in number, they crept back across the square and scampered up a wall to the rooftop. They leaped from that rooftop to the next and sprinted for an attic door.

Suddenly, four figures reared up before them in the moonlight, moving unsteadily. For a panicked moment, Leo thought they'd been caught. But the four figures had their backs to him, and they teetered like drunks.

Then one of the figures said in a young male voice, "Whazzat! I hear something!"

"I think it's my mom!" said a second.

The speaker turned and came face-to-face with Leo.

"Hey!" the young ape slurred. "Ish humansh!"

The gorilla lunged forward to grab Leo, but he slipped aside and the ape fell on his face. Leo sprinted for the door and kicked it open, then ran inside and down a flight of stairs to the top floor of the building. He heard the footsteps of the others following him. Behind and outside, they could hear the teenage gorillas shouting out an alarm.

Leo raced at full speed down a hallway, hoping the others could keep up with him. When the hallway ran into a door he kicked it open and ran into an apartment. Suddenly he was in a bedroom where a young female ape was standing over an old man ape who lay in bed. The male ape was snoring. Leo caught the briefest glimpse of Nova's familiar face, and then he was gone.

Out a back door and into another hallway, and then *crash* into another apartment where an old ape was pulling off his wig and false teeth. And then out onto a balcony, climbing over the rail and jumping across a short void to another balcony across the alley. Vaguely, Leo had the sense of the others following him.

Leo broke through another door and into another bedroom and this time the scene caused him to slow down. An ape child was putting a small human child into a little blanket-lined cage, and Leo recognized them both. The ape child was Thade's niece, and the human girl was the one she'd chosen as a "pet."

Daena didn't slow for an instant. She pushed the ape child out of the way and snatched the little girl from the cage. She was in motion again before Leo could protest. He started after her.

They left the ape child in their wake, howling in protest.

CHAPTER TWELVE

A squad of ape soldiers marched down the middle of the street with Attar at their lead. All of them had been roused from bed and none of them were happy.

The humans were huddled on the rooftop above them, waiting for them to pass. As soon as the squad was out of sight, Leo dropped catlike from the roof. The rest followed, one by one. Karubi came last. Unable to hold himself by his arms, he slipped and fell, hitting the ground hard. Karubi didn't utter a sound.

Daena helped him up and Karubi gritted his teeth. "Leave me here," he said.

"No," his daughter answered firmly.

Karubi gasped. "I'm tired, and just too old. Old men get scared."

"You might be old and tired, but you're done being scared," Leo said.

"Apes!" Gunnar hissed.

They all whirled around, but the apes were on them before anyone could react. There were two of them. A massive gorilla grabbed Leo's wrist, twisted it, and

72

plucked the knife out with stunning ease. The other stepped forward, and Leo recognized Ari's face.

"You are lucky I found you before they did," she said. She glared at them all, reserving an especially hard look for Tival. "Come back with me to the house. I can reason with them."

Karubi rubbed his damaged arm. "I've seen how apes reason."

Leo was about to ask how Ari had found them so quickly, but Bon stepped out of the shadows, not daring to meet their eyes. Leo wasn't sure whether to feel anger or pity for her.

"Is there a good way out of this city?" Leo demanded.

Ari said nothing, but Leo saw a hint of recognition in her eyes. Krull saw it, too. The big gorilla leaned in a little bit, casting a shadow between Leo and Ari. He growled to his mistress, "Do not get involved with these humans."

Bravely, Leo stepped into Krull's shadow and caught Ari's eyes, holding them. "You saved me today. Why? Why'd you take the chance?"

Ari hesitated a moment. "I . . . I don't know. You are very unusual."

"Like you can't even imagine," Leo said dryly. "Come with me . . . and I'll show you something that will turn your whole world upside down."

Daena gave him a sharp look. "So this ape will understand, but I can't?"

Leo ignored her and said to Ari, "You said humans

were capable of culture. You were right. I'll prove it to you. I can prove it beyond your wildest dreams."

Shouts drifted down the street, echoing off the walls. The noises were distant, but growing louder. Patrols were on their trail.

Ari looked at Krull and said, "When I was little I found a way to sneak outside the city walls. Where no one could find me. I can lead you there."

Krull shuffled from foot to foot and thumped a fist on his chest, but said nothing.

Krull stopped shuffling and eyed the little girl in Daena's arms. "This human child cannot survive the journey."

Ari seemed to agree with this. Her eyes flicked to Bon. "My servant woman will hide her in my house."

Obediently, Bon stepped forward and reached for the girl. Daena recoiled, clutching the girl to her.

To everyone's surprise, it was Karubi who broke the awkward stalemate between Daena and Bon. He stepped forward and scooped the little girl out of Daena's hands and into Bon's.

"We have to go now," Krull warned.

Leo nodded, and together the humans followed Ari and Krull down the street.

They ran for three blocks, hearing the sounds of patrols on distant streets. Harsh voices echoed over rooftops. But they saw no one.

On the fourth block, their luck failed. Several dark

shapes appeared at the far end of the street and one ape let out a furious roar.

"Attar," Krull said, recognizing the voice. "They've seen us."

"What are we going to do?" said Tival, suddenly terrified.

Again it was Karubi who took action. He put his good hand on Daena's shoulder and said, "Daughter—be well."

She turned, at first in confusion. Then she realized what he meant to do. "Father, no—"

"Don't worry," the old man said. "I'll be right beside you. Just like always. Hurry."

He jumped out of the shadows and charged straight at the apes.

Karubi forced himself to keep running toward the gorilla soldiers. He paused only long enough to snatch a wooden pole that lay in a doorway. He wielded it like a spear.

Attar and his apes watched as Karubi charged them. When he was only a few steps away, Karubi raised the pole in his good hand and let out a war cry, then swung it towards the massive ape.

Attar hardly blinked. He raised one thick arm to deflect the blow. With his other he clutched the old human by the throat and hurled him to the ground. Karubi felt the breath leave his body as the gorillas encircled him. Managing to regain his breath, Karubi sat up, staring up at Attar and looking the gorilla right in the eye.

Attar curled his lip. "Why do you not tremble before me?"

Karubi hesitated a moment and then smiled, remembering what Leo had told him. "I'm done being scared."

Attar frowned. This man seemed noble and dignified—Attar was not used to seeing this in humans. This human seemed enlivened by his defiance. He seemed . . . enlightened. Attar found himself envying that.

Attar looked up to see General Thade approach on horseback, his golden armor shimmering. Casually, Thade raised his arm. Attar caught only the briefest gleam of steel in the moonlight before Thade's sword came down and struck Karubi's head without a sound. Karubi fell with a thud. But Thade just studied Attar, trying to understand his lieutenant's hesitance.

Finally, he demanded, "Where are the other humans?"

Attar motioned up the street. "This way. They can't have gone far."

But when the two officers and their soldiers finished searching the street, they found no sign of the other escapees.

"They've disappeared," Attar said at last.

Thade seemed to agree. "Ring the city. Block every gate. When you find them, kill them all. But keep the troublemaker alive. I must talk to him before he dies."

Attar nodded, but did not move. He had something

else to say, something he did not wish to say.

"There is one other thing, sir," he said.

"What?"

"The . . . the senator's daughter. She was with them."

Thade's face froze into a mask of anger. "They took her?"

Attar thumped his chest nervously. "They . . . she was helping them, sir. I saw her myself."

Thade took a step back. Then he quickly turned Attar's statement to his own purposes.

"She had no choice," the general declared. "She was terrified. They threatened her life." Thade nodded, as though by convincing himself he had automatically convinced everyone around him. "I will report the matter to the senate myself." The gorilla warrior held up a gloved fist. "They'll beat their chests and beg for my help."

Attar nodded. "They are weak without you, sir."

Thade peered into the night. "Has she taken the old silverback with her?"

Attar had seen Krull before he'd ducked into the shadows. He knew the form of Krull well. "Yes, sir."

Thade turned a penetrating gaze back on Attar. There was history between Krull and Attar, long history. It meant little to Thade . . . unless it got in the way of his plans. "I trust," he said meaningfully, "that that will not be a problem?"

Attar straightened up. He hesitated for the slightest of moments. Then he forced the words through his teeth. "No, sir. As of now he is a criminal."

CHAPTER THIRTEEN

A house protecting the spring stood lonely and still in the darkness. Suddenly, something powerful struck the inside of the door, rattling the entire house. A second blow smashed the door to pieces.

Out stepped Krull, his old body still more than a match for the old door. Behind him came Ari, and then the humans. Leo walked a few paces out of the springhouse and then bent over, hands on his knees, gasping for breath. They'd run through the dark, near an airless tunnel leading to the house for what must have been an hour before they reached a set of stone steps that led up to the well.

None of them had had a chance to speak during the run—nor to think. But now, with the moon set for the night, they rested in the fields beyond the city walls.

Daena, who had held herself in check during their flight, now burst into silent sobs. No sound came from her, but her shoulders shook as she choked back her tears.

Ari walked over to her and put a hand on her shoulder.

"I . . . I am sorry. Your father was a brave man."

All the years of oppression and the indignities she'd suffered came rushing back in an instant. "You don't know anything about my father!" Daena screamed.

The human woman leaped for Ari, her hands outstretched. Ari stepped back, but Daena kept coming. The female ape bared her canines and slapped the human to the ground forcefully.

By that time Krull had stepped between them, looming over Daena like a mountain, and the other humans had gotten hold of Daena.

But Daena would have none of it. "Let . . . me . . . go!" she said, twisting free of Leo's grasp. She took off toward the trees.

"We have to go after her," Leo said.

"We have to be smart," Krull said. "Or it won't matter whether you catch up to your woman or not. Thade will be after us."

Leo followed Daena with his gaze, but then wrenched his thoughts back to even more pressing matters. He looked at the springhouse with its shattered door. "Will someone think of this way out of the city?"

Ari nodded. "They'll have to, when they realize we're gone. Someone will think of it. They'll follow the tunnel."

"No," Krull said. He strode over to a boulder nearly as tall as he was and began to push it toward the springhouse. Strain showed on his face, but the rock moved steadily until it blocked the doorway.

"Let's go," the gorilla said.

They raced after Daena.

Leo jogged next to Ari. "Krull . . . he's no servant."

Ari kept her eyes on the trees ahead. "Krull was a general. And a good one. But he opposed Thade, and Thade ruined his career. My father took him in."

"I'm glad he's on our side," Leo said truthfully.

As they reached the line of trees, a pair of yellow eyes peered out of a crack left by the boulder. Then a pair of strong hands began to push against the rock.

They caught up to Daena easily enough. Although she would not look at or speak to Ari, her only friends were Gunnar and Birn, and so she waited for them.

Too tired and too preoccupied with their private thoughts, they traveled in dark silence for hours.

Finally the sun began to lift over some distant hills, and the forest was filled with a pale light.

"Yeah, here it is," Leo said suddenly. These were the first words anyone had spoken in some time.

He stopped and pointed up to the treetops above him—trees with broken tops, and midtrunks blackened by a passing fire.

Leo followed the burn path like it was a beacon, until he came to the edge of the bog.

"This is where I flew in," he said.

The others, apes and humans alike, looked confused and unnerved by all the damage.

Ari said, "You . . . you did all this?"

Leo nodded. "My retro-burners." He saw that the

Captain Leo Davidson

Pericles and Leo give the thumbs up before the chimp's dangerous mission.

Leo crawls to dry land after a near-death landing. But what is this place?

The brave pilot finds out quickly that apes, not humans, rule civilization on this planet.

General Thade examines the new captives.

Ari has a soft spot for certain humans.

Birn will do anything to escape slavery.

The humans and their ape allies overcome fear and superstition on their journey to freedom.

Thade and his right-hand gorilla, Attar, fight for the superiority of apedom.

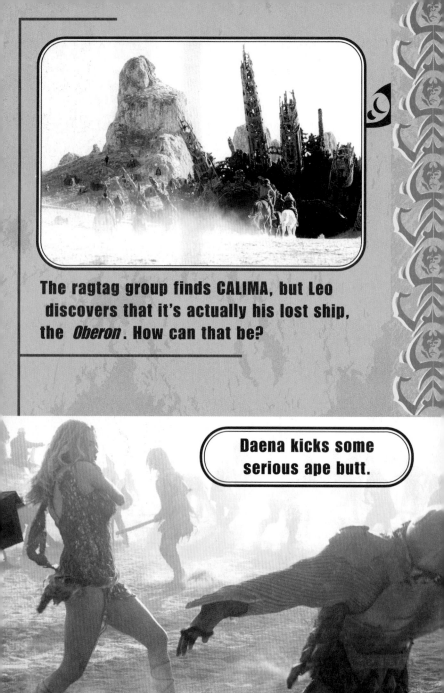

The ragtag group finds CALIMA, but Leo discovers that it's actually his lost ship, the *Oberon*. How can that be?

Daena kicks some serious ape butt.

Attar hails the return of
Semos . . . or the reappearance
of Leo's friend, Pericles?

Thade and Attar face off for the last time inside the *Oberon*.

With the balance of power thrown off, what does the future hold for the planet of the apes?

words meant nothing to her, or to the others. He added, "They're part of my ship. They help me slow the ship as it comes down."

Daena was fascinated by Leo's explanation. "I don't understand," she said, touching a burnt tree trunk. "You . . . you flew down from the sky?"

Leo laughed. "Well, *fell* down is more like it."

Krull gave a low growl that sounded very much like disbelief. Ari looked at her companion. "I'm sure he'll explain everything."

The former soldier grunted. "How can he explain what can't possibly be true."

Leo had had enough. "I'll tell you what can't exist," he said. "You. Talking monkeys. This whole place."

"He's insane," Krull said.

But Leo didn't care what anyone said. All that mattered was finding his pod, and finding a way out of this madness.

He walked to the water's edge and took a step in up to his ankles. Ari started to follow, but Krull held her back.

"What's wrong?" Leo asked.

Ari explained. "Apes cannot swim. We will drown in deep water."

Daena muttered, "That's why we pray for rain every day."

In the growing light, Leo spotted an oil slick. Without another word, Leo dived under the water.

It was cold and muddy. It wasn't deep, but it was cloudy, and Leo could just make out the outline of his pod, a white dome resting on the bottom of the bog.

On shore, the apes and humans began to shift nervously. Without Leo, they felt a bit lost.

"How long can a human hold his breath beneath the water?" Ari interrupted their thoughts.

Daena was not one to put up with anticipation for long. She dived in after Leo. After a few seconds, she, too, saw the strange pod. She stared in astonishment. She kicked her feet and reached out, touching the side of the pod, her fingers tracing the letters USAF without knowing what they meant.

Just then Leo came out of the pod carrying a metallic box. Leo felt something touch his leg and he recoiled, only to realize that it was Daena. He nodded to her, but her eyes were no longer on him. He turned to look in the direction her eyes were bulging.

A gorilla soldier stared back at him.

Leo started in fear, but the gorilla's face was frozen in a look of utter surprise, its eyes open and unblinking, its mouth open, too, and no bubbles coming out. There was another ape beside that one, and he was as dead as the first. They both floated in the water, but were weighted down by something. It gave them the odd appearance of standing on the bottom of the bog.

Leo slipped past the dead apes and pulled Daena after him. By this time Leo's lungs were burning, and he pushed up to the surface with Daena beside him. He swam until his feet touched the muddy bottom. Then he waded to shore, his clothes now heavy with water. The apes and humans stood dumbfounded, watching him, not knowing what to do as he knelt down.

"So you don't go near the water, eh?" he asked.

Ari shook her head.

"Then why," he asked, "are there two monkeys down there at the bottom of the bog?"

Everyone reacted in surprise, but it was Krull who raced first to the conclusion. "Someone else knows about you. And wanted it kept quiet."

Leo opened the box he'd taken out of his pod and pulled out a device smaller than a laptop computer. He flipped it open and began to power it up. He thanked the engineers who'd packed the emergi-kit to survive even a full-force crash landing.

Birn, unable to contain his curiosity, peeked into the metal box and began to pull out other items. He found a compass, flares, a medi-kit, and field rations in small metal bags. None of them made sense to him.

The small laptop gave a loud squawk. Humans and apes alike jumped.

"What is that?" Ari asked.

Leo began to tune the device. "It's called a Messenger. It keeps an open frequency with my ship so I can talk to them."

Ari came a bit closer, sniffed, and stared at the machine. "It . . . talks?"

"With radio waves," Leo said absentmindedly. He

waved at the air around him. "Radio waves. Invisible energy that floats all around us."

Krull leaned in protectively against Ari. "This is sorcery."

"Not sorcery, science," Leo said. "I just have to monkey with it a little. 'Scuse the expression."

Krull would have protested further, but the Messenger suddenly bleeped loudly. Leo didn't know whether to be surprised or delighted. "Contact." He studied the screen, and his expression became one of pure joy. "Jesus, they're already here."

CHAPTER FOURTEEN

Leo checked the readouts and even ran a diagnostic on the Messenger. No doubt about it. A signal was bouncing back to him, and from the frequency, it wasn't far away.

"Your . . . others like you, are here?" Daena asked. "Other humans like you?"

Leo nodded.

Ari scratched her head. "It's time you told us the truth. Who are you?"

Leo nodded, finally feeling that he was getting a handle on the situation that, a day ago, had spiraled into sheer madness. He said, "I am Captain Leo Davidson, of the United States *Oberon*. I come from a galaxy called the Milky Way. A planet in our star system called Earth."

Birn, who hadn't spoken at all since Leo had met him, said, "Is that far?"

Leo didn't know the answer, really. But he said, "Past any star you can see at night."

They all looked up. No stars were visible in daylight, of course, but each one of them tried to comprehend a distance that was past the blue sky, and past the sun.

"Your apes," Tival said, "they let you fly?"

Leo laughed at the sheer lunacy of his situation—a human asking him if monkeys gave him permission to do anything. He said, "Our apes live in zoos. They do what *we* tell *them*."

He ignored Ari's startled and offended reaction. He snapped the Messenger closed and said, "I'd call this hostile territory. So that means I've got thirty-six hours to rendezvous with my people. Then I get out of here and this nightmare is over."

Gunnar stared at him. "What happens to us? Where do we go?"

In that instant, a piece of the forest seemed to drop from the trees and land heavily on Gunnar. The human went down hard. The thing that had landed on him rose up, and the escapees found themselves staring at Limbo the slave trader. He had followed them through the tunnel to the spring house outside of the city. "You're not going anywhere," he said. "Several of you are still my property."

Gunnar struggled, but Limbo held him down with his foot. He slapped the human across the face. Heavy shackles appeared in his hand, and he managed to snap them around Gunnar's legs.

Birn bolted for the forest. But in the next instant his feet left the ground and he was hauled up into the branches by two of Limbo's handlers. Limbo laughed and strode over to Birn, holding another pair of shackles.

Leo watched it all calmly. He felt a little more like himself again. Finding the pod, and finding the emergency kit, had reminded him of who he was, despite the warped reality into which he'd fallen. He reached into the emergency kit and pulled out a standard issue sidearm. He released the safety. Leo would never point it at anyone, but he took aim at a tree branch near the slaver's head and pulled the trigger.

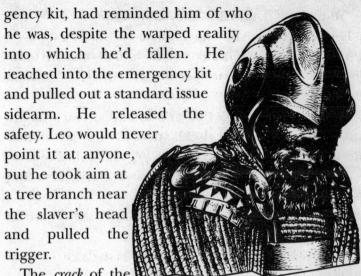

The *crack* of the bullet was a sound none of the others had ever heard in their lives. The branch by Limbo's head shattered. All of them dived for the ground, cowering. The two handlers dropped from the trees, beating their chests and backpedaling. Then they broke into a run and vanished into the forest.

Limbo stood as still as a stone, utterly terrified. Leo said calmly, "You saw what it did to the tree."

Limbo nodded. He dropped the shackles and helped Birn to his feet. "No harm done."

Leo said, "Play dead."

Limbo fell to his knees and put his hands up.

Daena had recovered from her own shock. Like Limbo, she didn't know what the weapon was, but she understood its power. "Kill him!" she said to Leo.

"Slave trader!" Gunnar yelled as he kicked Limbo. The ape fell over with a groan.

Ari had been watching in silence, but her empathy got the best of her. "If you kill him you'll only lower yourself to his level." Her eyes were pleading, and Leo was struck by just how human she could look.

Limbo grunted and stood up slowly, rubbing his ribs where he'd been kicked. "Exactly," he said. "She's extremely smart. You know I've heard her talking. Apes and humans, maybe there's something there." He took a few steps toward Leo, his toes curling in the dirt, as he continued to talk.

"Separate but equal . . . to each his own. It's a theory. It could work . . . "

He took a step closer and raised his hands.

Leo smirked at him and fired into the ground at Limbo's feet. The slaver jumped back in sheer terror. "Learn a new trick," Leo said.

Leo ordered Limbo to remove Gunnar's shackles, which the slaver did quickly. "Well," Limbo said, "I'm probably just in the way here, so I'll just get going."

Daena shook her head. "He'll lead them to us."

Leo agreed. "We'll make him our guest. Gunnar? Birn?"

The two human males took the shackles and hooked them onto Limbo. Suddenly the gun was snatched out of Leo's hands. He looked up to see Krull in the tree above him, now holding the weapon. The big ape dropped lightly to the ground.

"What the hell are you doing?" Leo demanded.

Krull hefted the weapon awkwardly. "You can turn this on me. I can't allow it."

Before Leo could stop him, Krull smashed the gun against a rock. It broke into several pieces.

"No!" Leo yelled.

Ari looked at Leo disapprovingly. "Who would invent such a horrible device?"

Leo was furious. In a single blow, his advantage over the apes had been reduced to scrap. "That device was going to keep me alive!"

"We're better off without it," Ari said.

Daena looked at Ari with undisguised hatred. "There is no *we* here."

Ari, her aristocratic sensibilities offended, wrinkled her nose. "Why are you being so difficult?"

Daena scoffed. "You mean, why aren't I acting like a slave?"

"That's not what I meant."

"Shut up!" Leo said. He'd had enough of all of them. "That goes for all species!"

Ari and Daena backed away from one another, with Daena sidling toward Leo. Her eyes shot daggers at the female ape. "You can't trust them," she said.

Leo shrugged. "You know who I trust? Myself."

"An admirable quality," Limbo said. "I find that works when all other—"

"You shut up, too," Leo growled. He picked up his Messenger and started off.

CHAPTER FIFTEEN

Gorilla soldiers stood in pairs on every street corner. Platoons of soldiers marched down the main thoroughfares. And not a single citizen complained, because last night a pack of humans had escaped, and (if rumors were true) they had kidnapped a member of one of the city's finest families.

General Thade had gone himself to Sandar's house to deliver the terrible news. Sandar had been nearly broken by it. Despite his disapproval of her activities, it was obvious that the old ape loved his daughter. To lose her to humans—the very creatures she sought to protect—was a devastating blow.

Thade had delivered his report with professional efficiency and then invited the senator to walk the city with him.

"If I ever thought that those . . . those creatures were capable of kidnapping my daughter . . . ," he mumbled for the fifth time since they'd begun their tour of the city.

Thade, walking tall and strong beside him, said firmly, "Don't blame yourself, senator. Your family above all tried to be compassionate to the humans . . . and look how they repaid you."

Sandar felt frail and weak. He felt old. He felt as though time had passed him by. Thade, on the other hand, appeared to be a pillar of strength. Capable. "General," Sandar said quietly. "Can you find my daughter?"

Thade stopped walking. He had known this moment would come. He had planned for it. He said, "If you untie my hands."

"What do you want?" the senator asked.

"Declare martial law," Thade said immediately. "Give me the absolute power to rid our planet of humans once and for all."

Sandar took a step back. The pillar of strength seemed to loom over him now. "I don't know—"

"Now is not the time to be timid and indecisive," Thade stated firmly. "I am the only one who can bring your daughter back to you . . . alive."

Thade waited. He studied Sandar.

The senator hesitated a moment. Then, as if frightened of his own actions, he gave the slightest nod of agreement, turned, and hurried away.

Thade watched him go. It was done. He would have his martial law. He would be the absolute authority on the planet.

Attar appeared at his side. He gave a salute and then said, "They are not within the city walls."

Thade rubbed his furred chin. "Hm. We underestimate this human. I will hunt him down myself."

Thade started away, but Attar said, "Sir, there is something else."

"Quickly, then."

"It's your father, sir."

Thade stiffened. "What?"

"He has sent word for you. You are to go. Quickly, they said."

Thade understood the meaning. He gave orders tersely. "Alert our outposts. Make sure the human does not pass."

Attar nodded. "I understand."

Thade caught his gaze and held it fiercely. "Except for my father, you're the one I depend on most. We are not just soldiers . . . we are friends, Attar. I'm depending on you."

It was a hard ride, but Thade did not feel a step of it. All that mattered was getting to his father's side before the end.

By nightfall he had reached the forest home of his father's retirement. It was a quiet place, a restful place. No place for anyone of their line, gorillas who had led armies for generations.

Thade's father's former profession did not match the vision of the poor, frail, gray ape that lay shriveled in a bed in this quiet country estate. But this, too, was his father, and as much as Thade wanted to turn away, he would not dishonor the ape who had taught him to be a soldier.

Thade knelt beside his father's bed. A single candle

burned in the room, keeping watch over the dying old soldier. The old ape's eyes were closed. The general reached out and gently traced the wrinkled line of that face.

"Father," he said softly.

His father opened his eyes and smiled weakly. "They said you would come tomorrow. I told them it would be sooner."

"Father, how are you—?"

"I don't have much time," the old ape rasped. "I . . . I've heard news." This did not surprise Thade. His father's network of spies had been the best in apedom in his prime, and was dependable right to the end. "Tell me about this human who troubles you."

Thade said, "He will be captured soon . . . and little trouble."

The old ape stared at him. "You're not telling me everything," the old ape said. "You believe he's not born of this world."

Thade was utterly stunned. "How can you know this—?"

"Has he come alone?"

"Yes," Thade replied, still dumbfounded.

"More will come looking for him," his father said definitively. Breath seemed to come slowly to his lungs.

"How?" Thade stammered. "How can you possibly know?"

His father took a deep breath, gathering strength. "I

have something to tell you before I die. Something my father told me . . . and his father told him . . . back across our bloodline to Semos himself." The old ape put a hand on his son's arm. "In the time before time . . . we were the slaves and the humans were our masters."

Thade snorted despite himself. "Impossible."

The old general raised one skeletal hand, pointing to an urn on the bedside table. "Break it."

Thade scooped up the urn and smashed it against the wall. Something hard and heavy clattered to the ground—a handgun. Thade picked it up.

"What you hold in your hand," his father said, panting, "is proof of their power. Their power of invention. Their power of technology. Against which our strength means nothing."

Thade hefted the gun. It had an interesting weight about it. But there was no blade, and it was far too short for a club.

"It has the force of a thousand spears," his father said.

Thade shrugged. "Then I shall summon ten thousand against it."

His father nodded approvingly. "I warn you . . . their ingenuity goes hand in hand with their crulety. No creature is as devious or violent. Find this human quickly. Do not let him reach Calima."

Calima. It was a name rarely spoken. "The ancient ruins?" Thade said. "Why would he even go there? No one goes there. It's forbidden. There's nothing there but some old cave paintings."

His father closed his eyes, but said, "Calima holds the secret of our true beginning."

"I will stop him, Father," the general vowed.

His father drifted back to consciousness for a moment. "This human has already infected the others with his ideas." The old ape gasped. "Damn them all . . ."

His hand dropped away from Thade's arm. His face settled suddenly into a relaxed pose, as though the pains of old age had been lifted. Thade frowned, whispered a prayer to Semos, and blew out the candle.

CHAPTER SIXTEEN

Beyond the bog stood a line of low-lying hills, some of them reaching almost to the height of mountains. The hike was not difficult, but the sun made the going hot. Daena, Gunnar, and Birn were best suited for the journey, and often seemed impatient with the others for slowing down.

Limbo complained for the first few miles, until Leo threatened to gag him with a tree branch. He was quiet after that.

Tival looked exhausted before an hour had passed. Ari was determined not to look like the pampered ape she was, and kept steadily in the middle of their small group. Krull simply endured.

Around noon they stopped for a brief water break, and Leo found Ari next to him, offering a canteen she and Krull had brought. He closed his eyes and took a swig, feeling the cool water wash dust down his throat. When he opened his eyes, Ari was still staring at him, her eyes so soft that it made him uncomfortable. After a moment, she broke contact and offered the canteen to Daena. The woman brushed it aside.

As they started walking again, Ari kept pace with Leo and said, "I have so many questions I want to ask."

Leo laughed to himself. "Get in line."

"What are these . . . *zoos* you speak of?" Ari asked. "I don't know that word."

Leo smiled. "Zoos are where you'll find our last few apes."

Krull grunted. "What happened to the rest of them?"

Leo wasn't sure how they'd react. "Gone. After we cut down their forests. The ones that survived we locked in cages for our amusement . . . or use in scientific experiments."

Krull said nothing, but Ari reacted with outright shock. "That's . . . horrible!"

Leo nodded. "We do worse to our own kind."

"I don't understand. You seem to possess such great intelligence."

"Yeah, we're pretty smart. And the smarter we get, the more dangerous our world becomes."

He said it because he believed it, but he also said it to break the connection she was trying to establish with him. Her eyes kept probing him, trying to open him up in some way, and even his harshest description did nothing to stop her. "You're sensitive," she said. "That's an uncommon trait in a male."

Krull had no patience for sensitivity or personal observations. He growled, "Why don't your apes object to the way you treat them?"

"Our apes can't talk."

Ari was surprised at this, too. "Maybe they choose not to, given the way you treat them."

Limbo, who hadn't spoken in some time, snorted. "Apes in cages. Right."

"Sounds like paradise to me," Daena replied.

The hills before them rose up to a steep slope, and humans and apes alike found themselves using hands and feet to scramble upward. Birn reached up for a ledge and hauled himself higher, his hand grasping on to some sort of handle.

He looked up to see what it was and found himself staring into the scowling face of an angry ape.

"Aiiyeee!" he screamed. He let go and tumbled backward, pinwheeling downhill until someone wrapped him in their arms and held him up. It was Leo. Calmly, the star captain pointed back up the hill. "Relax, they're not real."

A line of apes stood along the ridge of the hill, but they were effigies—"scarecrow" apes—nearly twice the size of Krull guarding the land beyond the hills against invaders.

Daena looked at the figures with a mixture of hatred

and fear. "The apes put those anywhere they don't want humans to go. Crossing that line means certain death."

Leo nodded upward. "What's so important on the other side of this hill?"

Krull said, "It leads to the ancient ruins at Calima."

"Calima?"

Ari explained. "Our ancient writings say Creation began at Calima. There, the Almighty breathed life into Semos, the First Ape, in the time before time."

Krull finished, "There it is said Semos will return to us one day."

Ari sniffed. "Of course, most educated apes consider such religious notions to be fairy tales. They are metaphors we use to explain our origins. I doubt there ever really was a Semos."

Leo started up the steepest part of the hill and casually passed in the shadow of the effigies. The other apes followed, with Krull prodding Limbo along.

Birn gathered his courage before anyone else did. He leaped across like a man jumping out of a frying pan and into fire. Gunnar followed, and then Daena. All three of them smiled.

The boldness of their act carried them up the rest of the slope. By late afternoon they had reached the peak. Leo took the group's first step over the final ridge and looked down on the other side. His heart sank.

Stretched out before him, as far as the eye could see,

were tents. He was looking down on a war camp of the apes.

The ape battalion had set up camp in the only likely crossing point in that region of the country. On either side, the hills rose up into even steeper mountain country. The only safe way through lay in a narrow valley carved out by a river.

The ape encampment stood on the near side of the river. Between the apes and the slope where the escapees lay hidden was a pen. Inside stood a small herd of horses.

From behind a tumble of rocks, Daena watched the horses in fear. "Monsters," she whispered.

"What are you talking about?" Leo asked.

Gunnar, beside him, pointed down at the herd. "I've heard they're possessed by the spirits of great ape generals."

"I've heard they eat human flesh," Birn said.

Leo rolled his eyes. These humans were more brainwashed than he could ever have imagined. "They're just horses. They'll do whatever you tell them to do," he explained impatiently.

Gunnar shook his head. "We should cross the river another way. Over the mountains."

Leo glanced up at the slopes to the right and left. Any detour would add days to their march. And if the Messenger's signal was accurate, he had one more day to reach his destination.

"I've got no time for that," he said. "We'll go through them."

Limbo, who'd taken as much abuse from this human as he could stand, hissed, "And where should we bury your remains?"

But Leo was already gone.

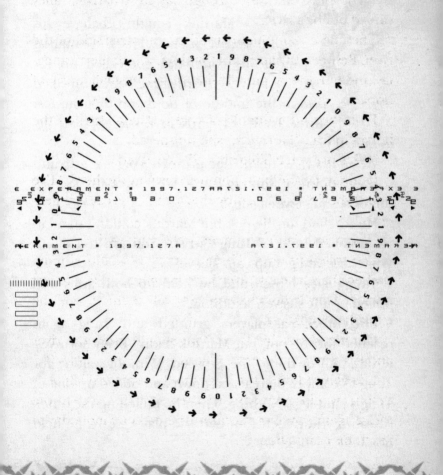

CHAPTER SEVENTEEN

Marduk couldn't believe his run of bad luck. First the battalion under his command got called up for active duty to guard some Semos-forsaken pass in the middle of nowhere; then he lost three hands of cards in a row to that big-mouthed braggart, Tuug.

When it was his turn, Tuug grinned a big ape grin and slapped down a winning card. He chuckled. "Semos smiles on me. I win again."

He reached for the pot, but Marduk couldn't stand it. He grabbed hold of Tuug's wrist. "You win too often. What have you got up your sleeve?"

Tuug's face tensed and he held up both arms and pulled up the sleeves. "Nothing."

The other cardplayers grunted and Tuug again reached for the pot, but Marduk hadn't been born yesterday. "All of them," he growled. Without waiting for Tuug to comply, he reached down and pulled up one of Tuug's pant legs. Nothing. Then he pulled up the other, revealing Tuug's left foot and the playing card he held between his toes.

"Cheater!" Marduk yelled. He jumped up and shoved Tuug backwards.

Tuug rolled over in the dust, roaring in anger. Commander or not, no one shoved him like that. He jumped to his feet, ready to do battle.

The sound of a galloping horse stopped him and the commander in their tracks. A rider stormed into their midst, leaping off his horse in midstride and landing among them as gracefully as a dancer but as solid as a rock. Marduk recognized him instantly as Attar, General Thade's right hand.

"Who is in charge here?"

Marduk straightened up. "I am, sir. They . . . they didn't tell me you were coming."

Attar scowled at him, delivering a look that indicated it shouldn't make a difference whether he was announced or not. "This camp is a disgrace."

Marduk gulped. Not a social visit.

Attar continued. "Some humans have escaped."

The battalion commander was relieved. Was that all? "If they come this way, we'll crush them."

"These humans are different. They travel with apes."

Tuug and the other started to laugh at the impossibility of the statement, but Attar cut them off. "You find this amusing?"

"N-no, sir!" Marduk nearly shrieked.

"I'm assuming command," Attar said. "I will personally make sure this camp is prepared. If anyone enters this valley, I want to know about it!"

• • •

The roar of Attar's voice could be heard almost all the way to the horse pens, where Leo was at that moment slipping between the slats of the corral and jumping easily onto the back of a dull brown stallion. When he tugged at the stallion's mane it turned on command. He grinned at his companions. "Who's next?"

No one moved. Leo frowned. "Then I guess we're saying good-bye here."

At his mild threat, Ari took a hesitant step forward.

"Wait!" Daena protested, pointing out to the river in the darkness. "You can't go. You're afraid of water."

Ari scoffed. "Well, you can't go, you're afraid of horses."

Leo trotted his horse forward and pointed at Daena. "You want to ride? Grab a fistful of mane and hold on."

He looked at Ari. "You want to cross the river? Horses are great swimmers. They'll carry you across."

Krull, as always silent until necessary, said, "You're assuming the soldiers won't tear you to pieces. I've just seen Thade's greatest warrior ride into the camp."

Leo studied Krull for a moment. "Sounds like he scares you."

Krull said, without ego, "I trained him myself. He should scare *you*."

Limbo rattled the chains around his hands and foot. "Well, good luck everyone, have a pleasant ride. Obviously, I can't go. So if you don't mind—?"

Leo surprised all of them by producing the key to Limbo's chains and unlocking them.

Daena appeared furious. "You're letting him go?"

"No," Leo said. "But he can't wear the chains if he's riding with us."

Limbo laughed. "There is no way . . ."

"Of course there is," Ari said. "You will ride with us. And if you try to get away, I'll tell Thade that we bribed you to help us escape from the city."

Limbo put a brave face forward. "I'll deny it."

"A very large bribe," Krull added dryly.

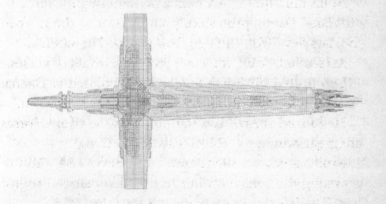

Limbo choked. "Of all the—one or two little indiscretions in my past, and they come back to haunt me!" He spat, "The whole thing's suicide! Ride through an army encampment? Only a human would think this could work."

Leo flashed a smile. He reached into the Messenger box and pulled out a device that look like the sidearm that had been destroyed. But this one was fitted on the end with a flare. "Attitude," he boasted, "is the first human freedom."

• • •

Attar had hours of work left ahead of him, but even duty was put aside to attend to his prayers. He knelt down on a woven tapestry in front of an icon of Semos. He bowed his head and began to pray. As always, he asked for the strength to be a better ape. He asked also for Semos to grant his wish to be among the first to bathe in the glory of the divine's light.

Attar opened his eyes, startled to find himself surrounded by unearthly light—light so bright it seemed to burn right through the canvas tent.

Stunned, Attar jumped to his feet and ran outside, half expecting to see the glorious figure of the Perfect Ape appear in the heavens, slowly descending, its arms reaching out for him.

What he saw was not nearly as personal, but still filled him with awe. A ball of fire drifted slowly across the sky. Small pieces of fire spat from the fireball's tail, wafting down on the camp like lazy fireflies. One spark drifted close to Attar, and he reached out for it reverently—but the spark vanished as it fell into his hand.

When his sharp ears heard the distant sound of thunder, he thought first of the ancient prophets who had foretold of Semos's return, predicting he would reappear to the sound of trumpets mightier than thunder.

Soldiers milled about all around Attar, but suddenly his military mind knew something was wrong. This thunder was the sound of horse hooves.

"Stampede!" he bellowed.

Even as he spoke the battalion's entire herd of horses came down the main avenue of the camp, scores of pounding hooves tearing up the soil near the riverbank. Soldiers scattered before them. Attar dived to one side as the first few horses charged past him. Rising to his feet, the ape soldier caught a glimpse of a human on a horse's back, and instantly knew that he had been fooled.

The soldiers were slow to react, but once they understood what had happened, they charged the stampeding horses with a vengeance.

Surprisingly, one of the horses veered toward the nearest group of soldiers. Attar recognized the ape as Limbo the slave trader.

"Help!" Limbo was calling. "Help! Don't hurt me. I'm on your side!"

Attar waved the soldiers on. Whether Limbo was telling the truth or not, if he survived the whole event, he would only make it that much more complicated, and Attar liked things to be simple.

The soldiers dropped to one knee and pulled back mini-catapults. Seconds later, the catapults launched fireballs of their own, fist-size balls of flame that sizzled through the air. One of them singed the hair on Limbo's neck.

"Hey!" Limbo shrieked. Instinctively, he pulled tightly at his horse's mane. The steed stood on two legs for a moment, then came to an abrupt halt.

"Move, you four-legged freak!" he cursed.

A soldier lowered a spear and charged at Limbo.

Leo saw the soldier and veered around, galloping past Limbo and slapping the ape's horse on the back. The horse reared and started forward again just as the soldier arrived, stabbing at the empty air.

Not slowing a bit, Leo raced by a watch fire and leaned over, snatching a firebrand from the edge of the flames. Then he hurled it into the nearest tent. By the time he'd wheeled around, the tent was already ablaze, and seconds later the neighboring pavilions had been lit by sparks, as well. In moments the camp was burning.

The horses reached the water and, hurtling in a mindless rush, plunged in. In the middle of the pack, the horses ridden by the humans and apes did not hesitate either. Tival, Birn, and Gunnar were across first, with Krull close behind and Limbo and Daena following. Leo was urging his horse to catch up with them now, but he looked back, realizing that Ari had fallen behind.

He could see her slowing her horse down as the river approached, the water lit up by the still-hanging flare.

"Come on!" he shouted.

Ari didn't answer.

Beyond her, Leo could see an ape soldier approaching, and by the broad shoulders and angry gait he could tell that it was Attar.

"Hurry!" he yelled, but still Ari hesitated. She was absolutely terrified of the water. Finally, her knuckles gripping the horse's mane until they were nearly white, she kicked the horse forward.

But at that moment Attar came within range. He raised his right arm and began to swing a bola around. The whir of its three weights began a high whistle, and then he released it. His marksmanship was perfect. The bola wrapped itself around the legs of Ari's horse, and the beast went down, sending the female ape sprawling into the sand.

From the far bank, Krull saw his young ward fall. He let out a roar of pure rage and frustration loud enough to shatter rocks.

On the near bank, Attar stopped, recognizing the sound of that voice.

That hesitation saved Ari's life. While Attar stood frozen, she scrambled to her feet and ran for a steep rock shelf at the river's edge. With nowhere else to go, she began to climb. Suddenly, Leo appeared at her side, leaping from the back of his horse to cling to the rocks just below her. He climbed after her for a moment, until they were twenty feet up, with the river bubbling below them.

"Ari!" Leo urged. "You have to swim."

Ari looked down at the water. It was terrifying to her, as deadly as quicksand.

"I can't!"

Leo spared a glance back and down. The warrior ape was moving with terrifying speed toward them.

Leo grabbed Ari's hand. "I won't let you go. I promise!"

Before she could protest, he jumped off of the side of the rocks, pulling her behind him.

● ● ●

On the far shore, Krull and the others watched help-lessly as the ape and the human vanished beneath the water's surface. Attar's soldiers reached the riverbank and began to launch fireballs into the water, but the missiles fizzled harmlessly on the surface.

While Krull watched the water anxiously, the humans grabbed the shackles they'd carried and approached Limbo again. But the slave trader, who had been licking the burn on his shoulder, looked up at them with an expression of sincere resentment on his face. "No, wait. There's no need for those now."

"Says who?" grunted Gunnar.

Limbo pointed to the burn mark on his fur. "Says them! They tried to kill me . . . like I was nothing but a miserable—" He caught himself.

Daena sneered. "Like what? Like a miserable human?"

The ape trembled—for once, his bravado and his gift for gab failing him. He said simply, "Please. I have nowhere else to go."

To everyone's surprise, Tival stepped in front of Daena. He said, "Then you belong with us." He reached out his hand and helped the ape to his feet.

Gunnar surveyed the scene—the apes on the far shore shouting in frustration but unwilling to cross; Krull scanning the unbroken surface of the water but failing to find any sign of Ari or Leo. Finally, he said, "We're the only ones who made it. I say we should stick to our own kind."

Daena agreed in her heart. Although dealing with

Krull and Ari and Limbo on a more equal level had opened her to new possibilities, she had to think of herself and her friends first. She said to Krull, "It's no use. Nothing will ever change."

"Look!" Birn yelled.

Rising out of the dark river, silhouetted by fires throughout the camp, was Leo. Clinging to his back was Ari. It was a shock to them all—a human rescuing an ape, an ape clinging to a human for support and comfort. It was a thing never before seen in the history of their world.

Leo staggered up onto the shore and then set Ari down, nearly collapsing from the effort. Krull rushed forward and gathered Ari into his huge arms, searching her for injuries.

Daena pushed past Birn and Gunnar to Leo, who was soaked through and shivering. He bore deep cuts on his shoulders.

"She hurt you," Daena said, touching the wounds.

Leo winced. "She was holding on pretty tight."

Daena carefully gathered a clump of leaves from the ground. She dipped them in river water and then slapped the matted leaves onto his cuts.

"I'm sure she was," Daena said. "I've seen how she looks at you."

At first Leo didn't understand her meaning; then he reacted with a start. "She's a *chimpanzee!*"

"A female chimpanzee."

Leo shuddered at the image Daena's words conjured.

Then he felt a sting from his wounds. "Ow. Ow! Is this stuff supposed to be helping?"

"These are goma leaves," Daena said, as though that explained everything.

"I don't care if they're potpourri," Leo said sharply. "They sure don't feel like they're doing me any good."

Daena pressed the leaves deeper into his wounds. "First your body will tingle, then you'll feel very dizzy . . . and then . . ." she said seriously, ". . . if you don't start growing fur, you'll be healed."

Leo started to react, but then finally caught the mischievous gleam in her eye. Daena broke into a full grin and laughed.

"Thanks a lot," Leo said. "I've seen plenty of unbelievable stuff today. The last thing I need is sarcasm." But he laughed, too.

Ari seemed to grow tense watching the intimate moment between the two humans. She bounded toward them. "The apes," she said, "will head downriver until they find a crossing. We should keep moving."

As the escapees set out into the night, they were watched by two pairs of eyes. But they were not the eyes of apes.

CHAPTER EIGHTEEN

Attar walked down the main corridor of the army headquarters.

He had returned to the city as soon as the sun had risen, to inform General Thade of his failure and the escape of the humans. He had ridden hard to bring the news, and he fully expected that every step of his galloping horse sped him nearer to his own execution.

As he approached Thade's office, the general stepped out and brushed past Attar, a grim look on his face. Attar whirled around and fell into step.

Thade said simply, "Where is he?"

Attar felt no need to mince words. "They crossed the river."

"You didn't stop them," the general growled. It was more a statement than a question.

"They were carried by horses."

General Thade stopped and turned to stare at his right-hand ape. His nostrils flared. "Horses?"

"Our horses, sir," Attar admitted.

The change that came over the general was as startling as it was sudden. One moment Thade was standing there with that cold, calculating look on his face. The next he was bouncing off the walls, shouting at the top of his lungs, tearing away tapestries, beating his chest in absolute anger. In a great leap he jumped up and grabbed hold of the chain that suspended a chandelier. He hung there, howling out his rage. As it swung beneath his weight, he drew his sword and slashed at it. The chain cut and the chandelier plummeted to the ground, shattering into a million splinters. Thade rode it to the ground. Then he rose out of the shards of glass and metal, once again fully civilized.

As quickly as it had come, his anger was gone. Thade looked at Attar and said, "Forgive me. I'm not angry at you, my friend. My father has been taken from me."

Thade wrapped Attar in his arms. Close as they were, it was the first time the general had given Attar that most familiar of ape sentiments, and Attar was both honored and startled by it. As Thade released him, Attar stammered, "He . . . he was a great leader. Your family are direct descendants of Semos. Now it is time for you to lead, General."

For a brief moment, Attar sensed some inner power in Thade, something of the blood of the divine Semos from whom he had sprung. But Thade did not speak the words of a messiah. Instead, he spoke the words of a general filled with his own ambition.

"Form the divisions," he said. "We are going to war."

CHAPTER NINETEEN

A mile or two from the river, the mountains gave way to more open plains. The escapees found a knoll where their campfire would be hidden from anyone on the flat land, and stopped to rest. The others settled around the fire and warmed themselves. Tival and Daena sat together. Gunnar and Birn slept. Krull, however, moved off into the shadows, his eyes scanning the terrain they'd already crossed.

Ari sat next to Leo, who watched Krull's back. "He'll stand like that all night," she said.

Leo nodded. "No question, he's army. I know the type."

Ari picked at bits of food. She offered some to Leo and then put a few small pieces into her mouth delicately. "Maybe we're more alike than you think." She looked up at the stars. "I'd like to see your world."

Leo shook his head definitively. "No, you wouldn't. They'd prod you and poke you and throw you in a cage, too."

"You'd protect me," she said confidently. She reached over and touched his arm.

Leo felt her hand on his, human and totally inhuman at the same time. Part of him recoiled at the intimacy in that contact, but another part 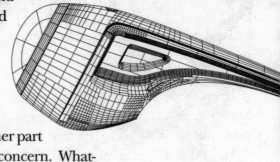 appreciated her concern. Whatever else she was, Ari was a thinking being, and she had developed an affection for him. And just maybe he had developed the same for her.

"You'd never be able to go home again," he warned.

She shrugged. "I can't go home now."

"I can't take you with me. You're right. We are alike. It's just as dangerous for you on my world as it is for me here."

Ari's voice trembled as she got to the heart of the matter that filled her with sadness. "I think after tomorrow, when you find your friends . . . I'll never see you again."

Leo clenched his jaw. "I never promised anyone anything."

Ari glanced over at Birn, and Gunnar, lying asleep around the fire. "That's not what they think. They think you're going to save them."

Tival and Daena sat far enough away that they could not hear what the ape and human were saying, but they could certainly see how close Ari had sat next to Leo. Daena watched the delicate way Ari picked at her food.

She took a hunk of dried meat and began to strip it away gingerly.

Tival, who as a slave had survived by reading people's moods, said, "It's not the way she eats, it's the way she thinks that pleases him."

Daena dropped her food and walked off in annoyance. She didn't want Tival to see how jealous she was. She *certainly* didn't want Ari to see how jealous she was.

Her life had not been easy, but it had been simple. Stay alive. But now there was this strange man from the stars, suggesting that humans could be more than the tribesmen crawling across the face of the planet. His voice and face were the keys that unlocked a hidden part of herself—desires for real freedom and for love.

She hated the fact that he had more in common with that female ape than he did with her. So what if she had grown up in a real society? So what if she had learned manners? She wasn't human.

Daena heard a trickle of running water and walked toward it instinctively until she came to a small spring winding its way down from the hills. She reached down to scoop up a drink and, in the moonlight, caught sight of her own arm. It was streaked with dirt and mud. She knew that if there were enough light, she'd have seen her face reflected in the water, and it would have been just as filthy.

No matter how much her tribe resented apes and their civilization, the apes, at least, were clean. She wondered what it would be like to truly scrub a lifetime of dirt from her body.

She stepped into the cold water and promised that a new woman would emerge.

The next morning, Leo awoke with a start, nearly forgetting where he was. The sky above him was wide and blue, and before him stretched a plain of short grass reaching out to the horizon. The others were slowly rising, too. Only Krull seemed to be fully awake, and Leo knew that the old warrior had not slept at all.

As he rose, he caught sight of Daena rising, too. She stretched, reaching up toward the ceiling of blue. For the first time, he noticed just how lovely she was. She smiled at him, and was amazed to see her skin clear and bright.

Ari appeared at his side. "We should go."

They mounted the remaining horses, some of them riding double, and trotted for another mile before Leo pulled out the Messenger and opened it up. To his delight, the signal was stronger than ever.

"Calima is not far," Krull said. "Just over that rise."

"They must be there," Leo guessed. "Maybe they're using the ruins as a landmark."

Leo galloped up to a small mound before them. Beyond it, the plain stretched flatter than ever, most of it hidden by a thin haze. Leo could just make out ruins rising lonely and desolate up from the ground.

"Calima," Krull said simply.

Leo activated the Messenger again, and this time the signal blared eagerly. Leo's heart jumped. His rescue team was close!

Excited now, Leo kicked his horse into a gallop and thundered toward the ruins. Quickly, a set of jagged towers rose up before him, set at an odd angle against a hill.

At the base of the ruins, Leo dismounted and popped the Messenger open again. The signal had reached its strongest pitch. Leo looked around, half expecting to see a pod or a landing craft, or crew members walking around a corner.

But there was nothing to see.

The others rode up to Leo, who sat staring at the Messenger in disbelief. What had gone wrong? Could it be malfunctioning? Could the location be wrong?

It was Gunnar who finally voiced the thought that smashed against the inside of Leo's skull.

"They aren't here," the human said. He paused, the realization gathering into frustration. "They were never here!" he yelled.

Leo said nothing. Daena looked at him, doubt creeping into her voice. "But . . . you said they would come for you."

Leo stood up, recoiling from the Messenger. He had clung to that signal like a lifeline. The moment he'd heard it, his world had returned to normal. The message it carried had been a thread spinning backward into the warp and weave of his normal life.

And suddenly it had been cut.

The panic that had gripped him in his first hours on this planet returned, and he felt a primitive need to run. Not knowing what else to do, he bolted into the ruins and

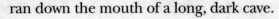

ran down the mouth of a long, dark cave. He ran. The sound of his own breathing echoed off the walls of the cave. He kicked something and tripped over it, falling to his knees. He looked down and saw something round and white sticking up from the floor of the tunnel. Curious, he scraped away the dirt and found himself looking down at a human skull half-buried in the dirt. He looked around and realized that the tunnel was littered with human remains.

Humans had been here.

But this was supposed to be the birthplace of the apes. Wasn't it?

Leo looked around. The shape of the walls bothered him. Or, rather, they looked familiar . . . and that bothered him.

Leo snatched up a human bone and walked over to one of the walls. He used the bone to scrape away the dirt wall. The soil crumbled away easily, and on his next scrape the bone tool scratched something metallic. Leo tore away more dirt with his bare hands.

As the dirt fell away, Leo found himself staring at a metal wall, and on that wall was the icon of the starship *Oberon*.

"Oh, no," Leo whispered. "No . . . no . . . no."

Leo held up the brand that the apes had burned into

him. The brand was a replica of *Oberon*'s insignia, only clipped and stylized.

The significance shook Leo to the core. He dropped to his knees, overcome by vertigo. If he had had breath in his lungs, he would have screamed. The tunnels, the walls, they were all familiar for a reason.

This was the *Oberon*.

CHAPTER TWENTY

Leo didn't know how long he sat there in the semidarkness of the tunnel. He was miserable. The ship that should be arriving to rescue him had somehow crashed here thousands of years before. That island of hope, the rock of rescue to which he'd clung, had sunk. It was now a ruin, the gutted tomb of his former crewmates.

Eventually, though, life roused him. He had been reduced to the same primitive level as the humans he'd met on this world, but like them, he resisted the urge to simply lie down among those old bones and die.

Leo staggered down the hall to a "cave" that was once a room. There were small caves set into the walls, and Leo knew immediately where he was. The Animal Living Quarters. Against one wall, Leo saw the remains of a sign that he had read either three days or thirty thousand years ago. It had once read: CAUTION: LIVE ANIMALS. But most of the letters had faded away, and only a few remained. CA LI MA.

Calima.

Leo staggered on.

Eventually, his feet carried him to a dead end. The wall before him looked like it was made of rock and dirt, but Leo knew that shatterproof glass lay somewhere beneath. With his bare hands, he chipped away at a section of dirt until he saw the hand scanner. On a whim, Leo blew dust off the scanner and pressed his hand against it.

For a moment, there was nothing. Then a sound whirred out of the scanner. The wall began to shake. Suddenly, it rolled back, shrugging off untold thousands of years of dust and muck.

Awestruck, delighted, and miserable all at once, Leo staggered onto the bridge of the *Oberon*.

Ari and Daena found him there, lost in thought. They moved hesitantly, as frightened by this place as Leo was warmed by it. They moved toward either side of him on the bridge, which possessed a light of its own.

Daena whispered, "What—what is it?"

Leo forced his mouth to move. "It—it's my ship."

Ari stood on Leo's other side. She said softly, "But these ruins are thousands of years old."

Leo shook his head. It was impossible. All of it was impossible. "I was here . . . just a few days ago."

Leo moved over to a control board—or rather, to a mound of earth that hid a control board. He dug away six inches of soil until the command keyboard appeared. Leo lit it up with a few touches. A date popped onto the panel-top screen.

5021.946

"Oh, my god," he breathed.

Leo worked the board. More lights went on all around the room. Ari and Daena watched as if in a dream.

Leo found the tracking lever and activated the scanner. On the small screen before him, he saw a graphic display of the current scan. The signal it displayed was the mate of the one picked up by his Messenger box.

"This is what my Messenger was picking up. The *Oberon*," he said to no one in particular.

But how could this all happen? What had brought the *Oberon* here? Leo had to know.

He moved to another section of the room and began to excavate, finally tearing away a chunk of rock to reveal a different command station.

"What are you doing now?" Ari asked.

Leo said, "I'm accessing the database. Every ship keeps a visual log—a way for them to tell their own story," he explained. "And maybe a way for me to find out what's happened to them."

"But it can't still work, can it?" Ari asked incredulously.

Leo shrugged. "This ship has a nuclear power source with a half-life of forever. In theory, all the operating systems should work."

Leo watched the board come to life and quickly summoned the data log.

The wall before them lit up, shocking and blinding everyone else in the room. This "cave" that had been dark for centuries was now bathed in bright light.

The screen sputtered and flared, not because it malfunctioned, but because the images in the log were disjointed or corrupted. The system automatically searched back for the next undamaged bit of information. It stopped, suddenly, and Leo found himself looking at Commander Vasich. But Vasich's face looked badly burned and scarred. Something bad had happened to the ship.

"*. . . we were searching for a pilot,*" Vasich recorded into the log, "*lost in an electromagnetic storm . . . when we got too close, our guidance systems went down.*"

"You couldn't find me," Leo said, offering an explanation that was several thousand years too late, "because I'd been punched forward through time."

"*. . . we've received no communications since we crash-landed. This planet is uncharted and uninhabited. We're trying to make the best of it. The apes we brought along have been helpful. They're stronger and smarter than we ever imagined.*"

Ari shifted uncomfortably at the sound of this.

The image dropped away into static and garbled viuals. Leo scrolled forward, looking for the next uncorrupted data file.

The static was replaced by the image of Dr. Alexander—but not as the young woman Leo had known. Her hair was now silver and brittle, and her face looked careworn. There were noises in the background like the sound of heavy hands pounding on a door.

"*. . . the others have fled with the children to the mountains,*"

125

she was saying. *"The apes are out of control. One male named Semos, who I raised myself, has taken over the pack. He's extremely brutal."* An especially loud boom made her hunch her shoulders, and her voice cracked, but she went on. *"We have some weapons but . . . I don't know how much longer we'll last."* Alexander glanced over her shoulder. A look of resignation settled over her. She was a woman who had just seen her own death and knew there was no escape. *"Maybe I saw the truth when they were young and wouldn't admit it. We taught them too well. They were apt pupils—"*

There was a sudden, disjointed blur, and four gorillas swept across the camera image. Dr. Alexander vanished without a sound. Then suddenly a large ape appeared directly in the camera lens and let out a massive roar. A hand covered the lens, and all images stopped.

CHAPTER TWENTY-ONE

Leo thought of the skull he had seen. It could have been Dr. Alexander's skull. Or the skull of her son or daughter, for all he knew.

"They're all dead because of me," he whispered aloud.

Ari put her hand on his again. "But we're all alive because of you."

Leo knew she was trying to make him feel better, but he glanced at her furred hand, and then at her, and he couldn't help thinking that the trade-off seemed miserably unfair.

He studied the readouts on the command console. "There's a little power left in one of the fuel rods," he observed.

Daena looked at him nervously. The words meant little to her, but the tone in his voice told her everything. "You're trying to find a way to leave us."

Leo swallowed hard. "I've been away from home for a thousand years."

He sat on the bridge of the *Oberon* for a long time. Decayed as it was, damaged as it was, it was still his closest

127

link to home, and he did not want to leave. He spent some time checking and rechecking the ship's diagnostics, but the truth was there was little to be done. What was damaged was beyond his ability to repair, and what was undamaged was ready to be activated at a moment's notice.

Finally, Daena appeared at his side again. She put a warm hand on his shoulder. "Would you come out? There is something you should see."

Leo hesitated, but Daena said gently, "This place has stood here for a thousand years. It won't go anywhere in the next few minutes."

Leo nodded and stood. He followed Daena up the corridor and out into the afternoon sunlight.

The landscape had changed. Where before it had been barren, now it was filled with human figures. They came in all shapes, sizes, and colors, dressed in rags, most carrying homemade weapons. All of them carried packs on their backs. Women toted young children swaddled in animal skins; men bore long, sharpened sticks like spears. And all of them wore, on their faces, a look of undisguised wonder.

"Who are they all?" Leo asked.

Tival spoke up. "Your story is spreading through the villages. They all want to see this human who defies the apes."

Leo shook his head. "Send them back."

Daena shrugged. "Back where? They've left their homes to be with you."

A few humans had been following the escapees on their journey—observing their brave escapades and reporting back to the human population.

Leo took a step out of the shadows of the *Oberon*'s entrance. As he stepped fully into the sun, the crowd spotted him. Instantly, a cheer rose up. It was a sound not just of applause, but of defiance, as well. Not just of joy, but also of courage. The sound reverberated in his chest, but he didn't know what it meant.

Not knowing what else to do, Leo walked out among them. Old men and young children reached out to touch him. On this planet of slave and enslaver, anyone who broke the mold was big news.

Just then Bon, the slave woman, appeared before Leo. Ari stepped past him and embraced the woman gladly.

"You survived!" Ari said. "I knew you would. You were always a crafty one. But what about the little—?"

"Here," her former servant said. Ari knelt down and smiled at the young girl Daena had rescued. At first, the youngster ducked her head behind Bon's knee. But then, as Ari cooed at her, she peeked out and smiled a shy smile. It was enough.

Leo looked at Bon, the servant who had been afraid to step out of her cage. He said, "You've been spreading the word. Quite a change for you."

Bon shrugged. "I was in that cage for a long time. It just took me longer to get out."

The afternoon was spent telling and retelling the story that few of the humans could believe. All that mattered was that somewhere in the galaxy was a place where humans did not live in cages, where they had mastered technology far beyond even the abilities of the apes. As he repeated this over and over, Leo finally understood the meaning of the cheer that had filled him with such emotion. To them he wasn't a star captain, or a defiant human, or even a hero. To them he represented a sense of something lost that lingered only as a memory—a sense of pride in their own humanity.

A sentry's cry drifted toward him. It was soon picked up by others as hidden watchers alerted the night-time camp that a rider approached. Leo and the others stood as Birn rode up to their fire.

"I saw them!" he said breathlessly as he dismounted. "Apes on the march."

"How many?" Krull asked.

"As far as I could see," the young man replied.

Krull scowled. "Thade has brought all his legions. That means the senate has capitulated. The general answers to no one now."

Leo had no idea how many soldiers Thade could gather, but if it caused that kind of concerned reaction from Krull, he was worried. He said to Daena, "Get your people away from here. They can go to the mountains, hide somewhere while there's still time."

Daena opened her hands in a gesture of helplessness. "They won't listen to me."

Leo bit his lip. He was responsible for bringing

these people into this savage existence. He would not be responsible for their slaughter, too.

"Okay," he said, thinking quickly. "If they came here to follow me, I'll let them follow."

The humans stood in a crowd, waiting for Leo to speak, to tell them what was to be done. He mounted his horse and chose his words carefully.

"This is a fight we can't win . . . break up and scatter," Leo urged them. "I'll draw them off. I'm the one they want. Let's go."

He spun his horse around and willed the people to do as he had asked them. Somewhere in his heart he knew that they wouldn't. After so many generations of slavery, the humans needed to resist.

Leo stopped as suddenly as he had started. He turned around and saw an awesome sight. The people had not moved. They remained silently as they had been, refusing to give up the little bit of hope they had gathered from this experience.

Leo galloped back to Daena. He didn't know if he was up to the task of leading a rebellion. He didn't know if his life was worth risking for a people he had never met before a few short days ago.

"They don't understand," Leo sighed to Daena. "It's over. Finished. There's no help coming."

Daena looked deeply into Leo's eyes. She saw the hero in him. She saw the spark he gave to her people, and she appreciated it. Daena touched her hand lightly to Leo's face. "You came . . . ," she said. She leaned in and kissed him.

CHAPTER TWENTY-TWO

The sky over the ape camp glowed red with the light of a thousand fires. In the camp itself, all was still.

Attar was first to sense someone approaching out of the night.

"Stop!" he challenged. "Come closer and identify yourself!"

A huge, hulking figure moved out of the darkness and into the light of a sentry fire. It was Krull.

"You," Attar growled. "You dare show your face here?"

Krull replied without passion, "It was not my decision."

Out from behind the massive ape stepped Ari, her voice thin but her frame erect and confident. "I wish to speak to Thade."

Attar sneered. "Impossible. You have betrayed your race."

"And you," Krull spat back, "have betrayed everything that I taught you."

The soldier in Attar bristled. "I could have you killed on the spot."

"You could try."

Ari stepped forward, putting herself between the two angry males. She pleaded with Attar. "Don't you ever think we apes have lost our way. Don't you ever have doubts?"

Attar raised his lip in another sneer, but this one faded away. It had seemed to him to be the will of Semos that apes destroy humans. But the night of the bright light had shaken his confidence. What he had thought was the return of his savior had been nothing but a trick. At first this had made him furious at the humans. But though General Thade was directly descended from his god, Semos, Thade had simply used the moment to further his own ambitions. With a brief nod, Attar allowed them to pass.

General Thade got word of Ari's presence long before she reached his tent. By the time she passed into his pavilion, he was standing with his thick hands behind his back, his face set in a reprimanding scowl.

"Why have you come?" he demanded as she entered. Outside, Attar and Krull stood like opposing forces of nature.

Ari said simply, "To be with you. Isn't that what you want?"

Thade understood her perfectly. "You are proposing a trade? Yourself for the humans." He snorted. "Even when you were young you took in stray humans. Your family always indulged your every whim."

He reached out, and Ari tensed. But Thade merely

flicked a speck of dust from her fur. "Now look at what you've become," he said disdainfully.

Ari knew this was her only chance. If Thade worked himself into a temper, she would never convince him. Desperately, she fell to her knees, submitting herself to him. "It's what you want, isn't it? I will be with you."

Thade looked away from her. "I have no feelings for you now."

He was disgusted by her seemingly boundless loyalty to humans. He had squelched his last bit of desire for her.

His eyes fell on a tripod of hot coals used to heat his meals. One of his servants had used a branding iron to stoke the coals, and the iron lay in the fire, still hot. Thade grinned evilly and snatched up the iron. "You want to be human?" he said in a voice harder than steel. "Then wear their mark!"

He grabbed Ari's hand and pressed the iron down into it. Ari screamed in agony.

Krull was inside the tent in a flash, but Attar was even faster. He appeared as if by magic between Krull and Thade, his canines bared. The two powerful males stalked each other for a moment, but Thade waved them apart and let go of Ari's hand.

Attar backed off and Krull rushed forward, helping Ari to her feet. Tears streamed down her face. Her hand still smoked where the skin had been burned. The smell of burned flesh filled the tent.

Thade sniffed it pleasantly. Then he said, "Let them go. Tomorrow they will die with the humans."

Attar motioned toward the door. Krull lifted Ari in his powerful arms and stalked out.

CHAPTER TWENTY-THREE

Leo emerged from the ruins to find Daena and the others waiting anxiously. He wished that he had better news for them, a better plan. He barely had a plan at all. All he had was a desperate hope. But it was something.

"There's one possibility," he explained to the humans who had traveled with him. "One shot, but it's worth taking."

He pointed to the ruins, where the tall spires jutted out almost sideways from the side of the hill. Those towers, he now knew, were the ship's engines. "We've got to draw them close," he said. "Put all these people behind the ship. But don't hide them. I want them seen."

"What about us?" Daena asked.

"You'll be on horseback," he explained. "In front of the ship, waiting for my signal. Absolutely still. You're the bait."

Birn looked determined. "I won't move until you say so."

"You won't even be out there," Leo replied firmly.

It took a moment for this to sink in. Then Birn protested, "But—"

"That's enough," Leo interrupted, and walked away.

He would not even consider letting a young boy get in the line of fire.

A short time later Leo was back on the bridge of the *Oberon,* syncing the command console up to the Messenger box from his pod. His only companion was Limbo. As a former slaver, Limbo did not feel safe among the humans, and had chosen to stay inside the ruins.

Leo had allowed him to remain only so long as he remained silent. But finally, the talkative ape could not hold it in any longer.

"Whatever you're planning," he said aloud, "don't tell me. The anticipation will kill me before Thade does."

Limbo hesitated only a moment longer.

"I can't stand it. You gotta tell me!"

Without looking up from his work, Leo said, "We can't stop them, but we can scare them. Scramble their monkey minds."

Limbo looked unconvinced. "We apes don't scare so easy."

Leo shrugged. "But when you do, it's out of control. You start running and never turn back."

The light of dawn crept across row upon row of armored apes, their breastplates polished, their spears like thickets on the plain, ready for battle. For a moment they stood as silent as legions of statues, staring at the ruins in the distance. At the head of his army, Thade knew the humans were watching from the hills. He wanted it that way. He wanted them to see the sheer power of apedom. He glanced at Attar and gave a nod.

The great ape threw back his head and let loose a war cry that split the air itself. Row by row, battalions of apes took up the cry, and buglers echoed it until the rocks shook beneath their feet.

As one, the ape army surged forward. Outrunners sprinted ahead, prepared to draw any surprise attacks from the humans, but quickly the main army caught up to them, moving with terrifying speed.

Around the ruins of *Oberon*, Leo made some last-minute adjustments to his Messenger box. Around him, humans muttered and shifted their feet. Some of them looked to the hills. Never before had they stood against a squad of apes, let alone an army. They were on the verge of panic.

But they were emboldened by the sight of a few figures riding out on horses. Daena, Gunnar, Krull, and Ari trotted out to the plains at the feet of *Oberon*'s ruins and stood there calmly.

Ari kicked her horse into a position beside Daena. The human woman glanced at her coldly. In response, Ari held up her hand. The brand scar was still red and throbbing. Seeing the mark, Daena softened suddenly. She reached out to touch the wound, but Ari closed her fist. She didn't want pity. She wanted respect.

Daena admired that.

The apes were two hundreds yards away, surging forward in a fast red wall. The horses began to prance nervously.

"Hold them as long as you can!" Leo shouted from the rocks.

Suddenly, another rider appeared out of the rocks. The figure trotted forward and took his place on the other side of Daena.

It was Birn.

"What are you doing here?" Daena demanded.

Birn stared out at the approaching army. "I'm part of this."

"Wait with the others like he told you!"

But it was too late. The ape outrunners were too close. Seeing the waiting humans, they hooted and surged ahead.

"Now!" Leo shouted. "Run!"

The humans urged their mounts into a run. They wheeled around and raced to safety, splitting into two groups. Birn, not knowing the plan, was unsure which way to go. His horse swerved one way, then another, and stumbled. The beast fell, pinning Birn beneath it. The ape outrunners shouted in glee and raced for him.

"No," Leo gasped.

He leaped from his hiding place and sprinted toward Birn. He reached the young man before the apes did and pulled him out from beneath the struggling horse. The apes were nearly upon them.

Leo practically threw Birn atop the horse and then sprinted back to his place. He had to reach the Messenger before he was caught. He jumped over a rock and touched a command button on the small keypad.

Nothing happened.

Leo touched the button again.

This time, his command was answered by a low rumble, like the sound of the planet itself rising from slumber.

The approaching army of apes halted, just in the shadow of the ruins they called Calima.

There was a brief, loud groan.

And then the engines exploded to life.

Flames poured out of the rocket engines, instantly turning the rocky hillside to slag. The first three rows of ape soldiers vanished behind a wall of pure fire, and the rows behind them were tossed into the air by a blast of heat with the strength of a tornado.

As quickly as it had begun, the rumble died down and the flames vanished. A forboding cloud of dust rose up, wafting across the plain.

The apes that had survived the blast staggered out of the dust cloud, choking and coughing. Two ape soldiers found themselves surrounded by humans who seemed to rise out of the ground. Instinctively, the apes growled, using methods that had cowed humans for centuries. But these humans only growled back, mocking the two soldiers. Their growls turned into a roar, and the humans charged. The soldiers vanished beneath the onslaught.

From their command position near the army's flank, Attar and Thade sat on horseback. Attar was sputtering and coughing in shock. Fire had poured over the legions like flames unleashed from the darkest pits of the underworld.

"How . . . how can there be such a weapon?" he stammered. "We cannot defeat them!"

Beside him, Thade sat as still as a statue. He watched more wounded apes stagger back from the battle line. Some screamed from the pain of their wounds. Others screamed out of fear and confusion. He sensed a panic spread through the ranks of his soldiers.

But still he sat, listening and waiting.

On the far side of the battlefield, among the rocks near the *Oberon's* crash site, the humans cheered. Even Limbo leaped up and down, hooting. "It worked! I'll gather their weapons and sell them for a fortune!"

Leo held up his hand. He, too, was waiting.

Thade waited for another moment, ignoring Attar's requests for orders, ignoring even the pleadings of his own wounded men. He forced himself to exercise patience . . . patience . . . then, when more precious seconds passed and nothing happened, he knew. He knew and he admired the bravado of the attempt. But it hadn't been enough.

Thade wheeled toward Attar. "We will attack."

Attar's eyes went wide in fear. "But . . . sir, he can destroy us all!"

Thade drew his sword. "We will see."

The general charged straight toward the humans.

Leo jumped up onto the rocks, staring out into a sea of dust. For a while there was nothing to see—just roiling

of sand kicked up by the blast. But then, out of the
cloud a figure emerged.

General Thade rode up to the shadow of the ruins,
staring full-face into the caverns out of which the fire had
come. Throwing back his head, he bared his canines and
unloosed a roar of challenge.

No answer came.

Ape and human alike had heard Thade's challenge.
More important, everyone had heard the silence that followed. Leo felt his shoulders slump. Thade had called his
bluff.

"By Semos, we're done," Limbo said, his joy turning
instantly to terror.

Thade stared defiantly up at the rocks searching for
the newcomer who had caused him so much trouble.
After a moment, Attar trotted up to his side. "I'm tired of
this human," Thade growled to him. "Attack!"

Horns sounded, and the rest of the ape legions
charged forward into the dust.

CHAPTER TWENTY-FOUR

Leo was scared, as scared as he'd been in his first hour on this planet. But he was also tired of trying to escape. If he was going to die, he wasn't going to die running from monkeys. Instead of retreating, he leaped off the rocks and into the swirling dust, sprinting forward in search of enemies.

An ape loomed up before him, stabbing at Leo with a spear. Leo kicked the spear away and rolled underneath the ape's outstretched arms. He snatched up the spear and kept running.

Another ape soldier sprang up, ready to cast a heavy net. Leo scooped up a handful of sand and hurled it into the gorilla's face. Then he plunged the spear into the ape's neck and snatched the net away.

Though Leo couldn't see her through the dust, Daena was fighting not far from him. She had long since overcome her fear of horses and now rode one like she'd been born to it. She wheeled around the ape infantry, using a long spear to batter any of the soldiers that tried to rush her.

143

spotted her from a distance. His hard, cold eyes
ed her pace as he drew out a bola and began to
overhead. When he was sure of her movements, he
le. ne bola fly. She seemed to sense it at the last minute
and swerved. The thongs did not wrap around her neck,
but one of the weights clipped the side of her head, and
she went down.

Daena was on her feet almost immediately, but her
horse was gone. She looked around for some means of
escape, only to find herself surrounded by apes closing in
on all sides. Daena drew a small knife from her belt and
promised herself to take at least one of the brutes with
her when she died.

Suddenly, a figure reared up beside her—a horse with
a rider. The horse dropped down, and Daena found herself looking at Ari's outstretched hand. "Come on!" the
female ape yelled.

Daena grabbed her hand and swung onto the back of
the horse—but it was too late. The apes had closed their
circle tight. One of them raised a spear . . . but suddenly
vanished behind a curtain of dust with a strangled cry. In
the next instant that curtain parted and Krull appeared,
battle-lust fully upon him. He roared an ancient battle
cry and charged the other apes, scattering them like so
many leaves. One of the apes slashed at the two women
and cut Daena's arm with a deep gash, but they managed
to gallop away. Krull smashed the attacker's skull into the
ground.

"Krull!" boomed a voice.

Krull spun around and found himself facing Attar. The surviving soldiers backed off as the two great apes circled one another. Each bore a sword in his hand. With lightning speed, Attar lunged. Krull blocked the thrust and slashed down, feeling his own sword clang against Attar's. Sparks flew from their steel.

Attar lunged, his sword stabbing at Krull's eyes. The old silverback slipped away, suddenly exchanging his brute strength for nimble-footed skill. As Attar stumbled forward, Krull spiraled his own sword around the other ape's blade and flicked it away.

Weaponless and outraged, Attar grabbed Krull's sword arm in both hands, struggling to break the older ape's grip on his own weapon. But even Attar could not loosen Krull's grip. So the younger ape sank his teeth into the silverback's arm. Krull howled in pain and shook his arm free, dropping the blade in the effort. With his free hand he backhanded Attar and sent the soldier sprawling.

Attar sprang to his feet almost immediately, and the two warriors circled each other again, stripped to the weapons they were born with—cunning, claws, and canines. Mad with blood lust, Attar sprang at Krull, who tried to beat him back. But the wound in Krull's arm was already slowing the old silverback, and though he landed a solid blow, he fell to his knees under the weight of Attar's body slamming against his own.

Attar's soldiers closed their circle to see how long the silverback would last.

While the battle raged outside, inside *Oberon*, on the command deck, an entirely different activity was taking place. Among the many systems Leo had powered up, one was the Messenger beacon that had first lured him to the ruins. He had never turned it off, and it had quietly hummed through a day and night without breaking the quiet rhythm of its search. No one had paid it any attention. Now, in the empty room, the scanner suddenly changed its tone.

Its ceaseless call out into the void was answered by the appearance of a tiny blip.

Thade waded through the battle, cutting down any humans who dared stand in his path. The battle had quickly become a rout. Savage humans were no match for disciplined apes, who were better trained, better armed, and stronger physically.

But Thade would not rest until he had one human's head on a spike, and he roamed this way and that, searching for the newcomer.

Amid the confusion he heard a voice call out, "Retreat! Try to get to the hills!" He grinned, recognizing the voice of the human he sought.

He was even more satisfied when another human replied, "They cut us off! We're trapped!"

The humans had formed a tight circle, their primitive weapons facing outward, as the apes closed in around them. It was a hopeless cause. The apes outnumbered them three to one and fought with iron weapons, while the humans held only sharpened sticks. But they looked defiant.

Thade was ready to make the death blow. He spotted Leo in the fray and charged full speed at the defenseless human.

Leo's face was grim. He knew Thade could tear him to pieces. He didn't care. Something primeval answered the challenge Thade uttered, an instinct so base it could hardly be called human. Here was one primate challenging the right of another, and Leo would not, could not, ignore it.

Thade threw himself forward with blinding speed. Leo sidestepped and kicked the soldier, feeling his foot clang on Thade's shirt of armor. But he quickly followed with a punch that snapped Thade's head to the side. If not for the general's incredibly thick neck, the blow might have broken his jaw.

Thade's counterattack was faster than lightning. He delivered a backhand that drew blood from Leo's mouth. Leo stumbled backward, fell, and then rolled to his feet. But Thade was already on him, punching Leo in the stomach and dropping the human to his knees.

Thade raised his fist to finish the impertinent human.

The raising of his hand seemed like a magical gesture, calling down thunder, for as his fist went up, a deafening sound shook the sky. Startled, ape and human alike looked up. A white streak flashed across the sky, then arced around and slowed, heading straight for them.

"By Semos, what is it?" Attar asked.

Leo looked up and struggled to understand. A spark of recognition crossed his face and he smiled down at the ground. He knew what it was.

The white pod circled the battlefield in a lazy arc, then settled down to the ground, kicking up small clouds of dust as it came to a stop right in front of the ruins.

Not a figure moved. Neither ape nor human dared speak or breathe. Even Thade paused in midstrike, his hand still poised in the air.

The pod's hatch opened with a small hiss. From inside the pod came a steady beeping sound that matched the pattern on *Oberon*'s screens. Everyone took a step back, terrified.

Then a hand slowly emerged from the pod—an ape's hand.

A chimpanzee stepped out of the pod, blinking in the sunlight. Around him, dust and light swirled, mimicking exactly the religious icon Leo had seen several times.

"Semos."

CHAPTER TWENTY-FIVE

Attar said it. His jaw had dropped, his eyes wide with amazement. Without hesitation, he dropped to his knees. "Semos."

"Semos . . . Semos . . ." The word passed like a breeze through the ranks of ape soldiers. "Semos!"

Attar turned to Thade, who stood over Leo, looking suspicious and angry at this impossible new arrival.

"Sir!" Attar said. "The prophecy is true. Semos has returned to us."

Thade did not move. Leo did. As the general's attention was turned away, he jumped to his feet and bolted right for the pod. As one, the apes cried out in alarm, but then to their utter amazement "Semos" opened his long arms and jumped into Leo's embrace.

"Pericles!" Leo laughed.

The chimp hugged Leo and then held up one of his hands. The thumb was extended. Leo laughed again and gave a thumbs-up sign of his own.

"Good boy. You brought your pod home."

Suddenly, the humans erupted in cheers. The figure of

sorcery, whoever he was, had obviously come to help Leo. Their shouts electrified Leo. Quickly, he unhooked a survival pack from Pericles' back and slung the backpack over his own shoulders.

"Okay, Pericles," he said, "let's go explain evolution to the monkeys."

Boldly, Leo marched toward the apes. As he approached, soldiers tossed their weapons aside and dropped to their knees.

Thade looked at them with sheer hatred in his eyes. "Stop them!" he ordered, but not a single ape obeyed. In fact, as Leo neared, they backed away, awestruck and terrified.

"Go back!" Thade ordered. "I order you . . . hold your positions. Cowards!"

No one listened to him. The humans cheered as apes continued to back away; then the apes broke into a run. "No . . . ," Thade growled. "No!"

He sprang into Leo's path. With one violent blow he struck Pericles out of the human's hands. The spectators gasped in shock.

Thade leered down at Leo. "Wherever you come from . . . you're still just a wretched human!"

Thade gathered up a handful of Leo's shirt, lifted him into the air, and then tossed him a dozen yards away. He hit the ground hard, and the backpack skittered away. He tried to stand up, but Thade was on him again, lifting and tossing once more in an act of pure and primitive rage. Leo landed near the entrance to *Oberon*. Thade slapped the human, and Leo staggered backward, into the tunnel itself, still clutching for the backpack. He ran partway down the tunnel, hoping to open the pack, but Thade kept him off balance, driving him down the tunnel.

"I will bury your remains . . . so they can be forgotten like the rest of your stinking race," Thade promised.

Leo backpedaled until he was through the security doors and on the bridge. Only then did he have time enough to rip open the pack. He jammed his hand inside and pulled out the object he sought.

His hand came out holding the gun. He leveled the weapon at Thade. To his surprise, Thade saw the gun and froze in fear.

Leo was shocked. "You know what this is."

Thade took a step back. This was the thing his father had warned him about, the device that could turn these ridiculous weak-limbed humans into masters of the planet. The ape general had no idea what to do next, when fate intervened on his behalf. Ari ran into the cave, looking for Leo. In an instant Thade was on her, his arms grabbing her and holding her like a shield between his body and the weapon.

"Let her go!" Leo demanded.

Thade grinned and put a powerful hand on her throat. "I am willing to die. Are you willing to see her die?"

Leo hesitated. The answer was no, and he knew it. He was not a good enough shot to kill Thade without risking

Ari's life, and if he missed, the ape would snap her neck. Slowly, he set the gun on the ground and then kicked it over to Thade.

The gun skittered on the ground and was stopped by the foot of Attar, who had entered the room in pursuit of his general. Attar lifted the gun curiously.

"Attar," Thade said, "with that device they are no longer the weaker race. We cannot allow it."

Leo said in reply, "Look around you. This is who you really are. We brought you here. We lived together with you in peace . . . until Semos murdered everyone."

"No," Attar said in a low voice. "Semos, a murderer?" He looked around at this cave of wonders and then looked at Thade. "Can this be true?"

Thade said only, "They'd make us their slaves. Bring me the gun!"

Attar hesitated a moment. Then he held out the gun for Thade. The general threw Ari to the floor and snatched the weapon away. His long finger curled around the trigger.

Thade laughed. "Does it really make a difference how we arrived here? We are the only ones who will survive."

Ari looked pleadingly at Thade. "Please don't hurt him."

Thade cocked his head in a quizzical look. Instead of

pointing the gun at Leo, he leveled it at Ari. "I was always less than human to you. Someday, if humans are even remembered, they will be known for what they really are. Weak and stupid."

He pulled the trigger.

Nothing happened.

"What?" he grunted. He pulled the trigger again, but the gun was lifeless.

Leo grinned. "Stupid people. Smart guns."

Thade motioned to Attar. "Kill them."

Attar did not move.

The general bristled. "I am your commander. Obey me!"

But his loyal officer only stared back at him, his black eyes burning into Thade's.

Attar's lips curled back instinctively, showing his fangs. "Everything I have believed in . . . is a lie. You knew about this place. You and your family have betrayed us. I will not follow you anymore."

Leo slowly drifted toward the door, closer to where Ari and Attar stood. He reached the control panel.

Thade spotted the human and tried to freeze him in place with a glare. "When you're dead and this place buried beneath the rocks, no one will know the truth."

"You will," Leo said. "Forever."

He slapped his hand to the wall. Thade had no idea what his gesture meant—not until Leo reached forward and grabbed Ari's hand, practically pulling her through the air and out into the tunnel. As he did, the shatter-proof glass doors of the bridge began to close.

Thade watched the doors close for a moment, still not comprehending. But a second later his calculating mind understood the idea of doors that closed by themselves, and he knew that a gate that closed by Leo's command might only open by it. He leaped nearly across the room and slammed himself against the door just before it closed. He managed to wedge his hands between the

door and the wall. The servos whined, trying to finish their locking procedure. Thade howled, his massive arms straining. With unbelievable strength, the ape began to roll the glass doors back.

Suddenly, two more hands appeared at the door. Attar's hands, even larger than Thade's, settled over the general's wrists.

"Help me . . ." Thade gasped from the effort. "—my friend. I command you . . ."

But Attar said only, "I will pray for you."

With all his strength, Attar hurled Thade back into the room. And then the doors shut between them.

Thade threw himself at the barrier with the force of a hurricane. But the shield was designed to withstand the pressures of an implosion, and not even that terrifying ape could break it. The human and the two apes watched impassively as Thade smashed himself time and time again against the wall. Then, giving up, he turned his fury on the control panels, ripping them to pieces. The same rage that Attar had seen earlier filled Thade again. It was terrifying to behold, and Leo understood how the ship-wrecked humans had grown to fear the apes.

CHAPTER TWENTY-SIX

Attar himself placed the last stone atop Krull's grave. Of all the violent deeds he had committed in Thade's name, this was the one he would regret most. Krull had earned a warrior's death, but not at the hand of his best student. It was a murder that Attar would carry with him to his own grave.

Ari knelt by the old silverback's grave. A tear spilled from her eye as she whispered, "All the years you put up with me . . . this time I wish I could've protected you."

Leo put a hand on her shoulder. She gave one last sob, then rose and faced him. Leo was holding Pericles. The chimp had been weak and scared since Thade's blow, but he would heal. The human handed him to Ari.

"Now you have someone to take care of," he said to her. "Do a good job. He means a lot to me."

Ari nodded. "I can promise you I won't put him in a cage."

Attar looked at Pericles, his eyes still haunted by the thought that this might be his savior. And, of course, in some ways it was—but as the ancient teachings themselves foretold, true wisdom came from within, and the arrival of his divine hero had only taught Attar that he needed to save himself.

Attar looked out across the battlefield. Under the shadow of the ruins, hundreds of graves had been dug, marked only by simple stones.

Attar said, "We will leave the graves unmarked. No one who comes here will be able to tell ape from human. They will be mourned together . . . as it should be from now on."

Leo held up his Messenger box, which was now tuned to the frequency in *Alpha Pod*. It had started to beep a half hour ago. "It's found the coordinates of the storm that brought me here," he explained. "I have to go."

"It would mean a great deal to everyone," Ari said, "it would mean a great deal to me . . . if you would stay."

Leo shook his head. "I have to leave now. I have to take a chance that it can get me back. I have a home to go to."

They walked with him to *Alpha Pod*, where some of the other humans had gathered. As they arrived, Ari said softly, "One day they'll tell a story about a human who came from the stars and changed our world. Some of them will say it was just a fairy tale, that he was never real." She choked back a sob. "But I'll know the truth."

She embraced him quickly and then let go.

The proximity alert had become more urgent, and Leo was about to enter the pod when he spotted Daena. She stood with Gunnar and Birn. The two men waved to him, but Daena remained motionless. Leo ignored the pod's alarms and ran over to her. As he did, she broke into an expression that held both smiles and tears, and the woman practically threw herself into his arms. He held her tightly, as he had never been able to do.

"You know I can't take you with me," he said.

She nodded, pressing her face against his shoulder. "Then you'll have to come back."

She looked up and surprised him with a kiss. It was long and tender, softer than he ever would have expected from that wild woman. When she broke away, she did not wait, but turned and ran into the rocks where she would not see him leave, and no one could see her cry.

Leo gave one last wave to the humans and apes assembled around him. Then he ducked into the pod. He sat down in the pilot's chair and slipped on the control helmet.

"Close pod," he sad.

The hatch sealed itself shut.

And suddenly he was all pilot again, surrounded only by the instruments and controls of a ship he had been trained to fly. He ran through flight checks quickly, easily, almost as though what had just happened had never been, and in a moment the pod was rising into the air and rocketing past the reach of the planet's gravity.

But of course it had happened, in all its sheer terror and wonder. He would miss Ari, and he would miss Daena and Birn. But that place was not his home.

Leo called up a star chart and tried to map his coordinates, but the star navigator bleeped and returned a simple message: COORDINATES UNKNOWN.

"No kidding," Leo replied.

Leo banked the ship along the gravity well of the planet of the apes and curled up into outer space. Before him, the endless bright cloud of the electromagnetic storm appeared, just as he had seen it before. Leo set a course full-speed for the center of the storm. He didn't know what would happen to him this time. But nothing could be worse than what he had been through, and nothing could be better than home. Home was worth the risk.